THE PRESIDENT'S PAPERS

Pedro Vargas

ISBN-10: 0989687619
ISBN-13: 9780989687614

PROLOGUE

Luis Martinez was a local. He had been flying for a little over three years. At this particular moment he was anxious to take off because it was getting dark soon, and to complicate matters, it seemed that there was going to be a rain squall that he wanted to avoid badly. The reason he was so anxious to avoid the bad weather was that unbeknownst to the Agency, Luis had managed to obtain employment as a pilot through the recommendation of a friend who had not been aware that Luis had only minimal training in instrument flying. He had been lucky. He had not been required to fly in really bad weather, until now. Visibility was going to be cut drastically if he didn't take off soon, and therefore the reason for the nervousness. He glanced at his watch as he took a drag on his cigarette. Only an hour of sunlight left and it looked like the rain was moving in quickly. Shit! This was going to give him an ulcer. He crushed the cigarette with the heel of his shoe, and went to see what was causing the delay.

Twenty minutes later Luis was in the air and his worst fears were realized. It was dark, raining, and cloudy. Wind gusts were buffeting the little Cessna Skyhawk at unexpected moments making it dip suddenly and giving him a sinking feeling in the pit of his stomach. The windshield blades struggled to keep up with the intense rain, but it was a losing battle, visibility was nil. He tried to rise above the clouds to avoid the worst of the weather but the plane did not have enough ceiling. In spite of all this it seemed that the plane was holding its own. He was comforted by the steady drone of the single engine and the muted repetitive clicking of the windshield wipers. It seemed that even with the apparent danger, it was turning out to be a routine flight after all. He was just beginning to feel at ease when suddenly, a brilliant white flash filled the cabin followed by a horrendous crashing sound. After a few seconds of disorientation, Luis realized that the plane had been struck by lightning. He moved the yoke and realized to his satisfaction, that the plane still responded, but after a complete review of the plane's instrument panel, he realized with a shock, that his artificial horizon, altimeter, and all other electronics had stopped working. Everything had been knocked out by the strike. Immediately, perspiration started to bead on his forehead, and his mouth dried up. He was traveling blind through white cloud swirls. He strained to see a break in the clouds and could not. After a few tense minutes of blind flying, he finally broke through the cloud cover only to see lights overhead. Puzzled, he looked at his instruments and to his horror realized that somehow he had turned the plane and had been flying upside down. In a panic, he righted the plane and tried desperately to gain altitude. Suddenly, a large mass loomed ahead of him. With a sickening realization, he realized he was approaching a mountain and the last thing Luis saw in his life was the stark rock background of the mountain face looming ever faster toward him and then everything went black.

THE PRESIDENT'S PAPERS

This was, on the face of it, an isolated small plane crash. Little could anyone have foreseen that it would trigger a series of events that would follow each other in rapid succession, and like a row of falling dominoes, would inevitably culminate in a situation that would eventually threaten the security of the United States.

1

I looked out at the world at 32,000 feet. Everything looked life-less and ethereal, the steady hum of the plane the only indi-cation of reality. Falling back on my headrest I closed my eyes. Robert, Robert, Robert! Opening my eyes, I looked at the manila folder in my lap, the life and times of my mentor, my friend, re-duced to eight double spaced printed pages, a few photographs, and officially stamped and approved copies of different assorted documents. There was no immortality in the Company. Here one day, and gone the next. The station chief in England would say, "Did you hear about Robert? Too bad, what a pity.", and that would be all the eulogy offered.

I was to be the cleanup man. My job would be to make sure that all earthly remnants of the deceased were ferreted out, classi-fied, bagged, and after careful evaluation and scrutiny, destroyed. These earthly remains resided at present, at Tamarindo beach, a secluded spot near Guanica bay on the southeastern coast of the island of Puerto Rico.

Robert had been assigned to that area many years back, to stop a transfer of U.S. nuclear sub plans, an exchange that was to take place between a Chinese *Guoanbu* agent and a Soviet KGB agent. The latter was to come in on a clandestine boat from Cuba. As Bob enjoyed telling it, after arriving at the San Juan international airport, and after several stress relief drinks at a bar at the terminal, he had driven from San Juan in a rental car to his assignment, passing by the sweeping Guanica bay and had continued several miles on the meandering bay side road that threaded up the side of a mountain through Puerto Rico's only desert habitat. He drank in the unique rugged, dry landscape and fell in love with it. Glancing to his right he could see the startling contrast of the beautiful searing blue water with the glitter of the Caribbean sun reflecting off of the waves of the bay hundreds of feet below and to his left the cacti, sea grapes, and the other abundant but dried out vegetation typical of this region. After about a half-hour drive he had come to a seaside hotel called Copamarina, a tropical little jewel with rooms that overlooked the bay. You could step from your room directly onto the beach. It was the perfect retreat. He took in the majestic palms swaying in the breeze, and the lush tropical landscape and he decided instantly to make this his base of operations for the next few weeks. With plenty of time on his hands, at the first chance he got, he had continued his exploration of both sides of the seaside road, taking a drive further down the coast, and discovering that traveling westward the road went past a large public beach called *Cana Gorda* which he later discovered to mean *Thick Cane,* an allusion to the vast sugar cane fields that were present towards the entrance of the bay area. The public beach always seemed to be full of a mixture of locals and adventurous tourists seeking to discover the "real" Puerto Rico. Traveling towards the east he came to a public beach that was even more isolated called *Tamarindo*. The road seemed to end here, but if you walked further up, following the coastline, you crossed the wide expanse of sand that served as a parking lot under the shade of pine tree clusters and palms, you could just barely discern that the road did indeed continue, although only faintly observable, basically as a dirt trail. The trail was overgrown with vegetation. Bob had followed the trail choosing to leave his vehicle at the sand parking area, and had proceeded on foot and discovered yet another stretch of untouched beach far from the prying eyes of the public. He felt it was his personal oasis and immediately claimed this in his heart, as his own, even though he didn't know who owned that location. He subsequently found out that all beachfront property in Puerto Rico was owned by the local government and thus public, but by pleading with the office he somehow managed for the Company to convince the local government to declare this sector a wildlife habitat area, probably in exchange for favors he never disclosed to me, and which I preferred not to know about anyway, and had a barricaded gate erected with large NO TRESPASSING signs, and signs from the Wildlife Commission declaring the area a protected natural habitat. He next had a two-story frame building built beach-side with a wraparound screened porch, and even had a small airstrip built next to that. He made this his base of operations for his Caribbean domain. He had more than $100,000 of communications and computer equipment installed which he obtained from a bureau that questioned the purchase of a box of Kleenex. How he did it I don't know. After some time it was finished to his satisfaction. He loved the place, he absolutely loved it. As to the original assignment that had brought him there in the first place, Bob had ascertained the exact whereabouts and identity of the Chinese agent. He had arranged for the Chinese agent to be put on a container vessel bound for Hong Kong, after knocking him out with chloral hydrate, mixing the powerful hypnotic into one of the drinks he had ordered at the local hotel he was staying at. The nuclear sub plans had been retrieved, and for all I know, the Soviet agent was still waiting for them.

Following that little caper, Bob left his new Caribbean base of operations only when he absolutely had to on extended assignments. Precisely a short time after he had settled in, he was assigned, as one of his tasks from his new location, to monitor some questionable activity at the University of Puerto Rico. Unfortunately for him, this task turned into a very extended one, in which he was temporarily deprived of enjoying his beachside paradise to the fullest, simply because of the fact that he met me.

I was an Army brat, my father had moved from base to base in several different states until he finally ended up stationed at the Roosevelt Roads Army base. I was about to start university studies. My mother was Puerto Rican, and thus under her tutelage I became fluent in Spanish and I spoke it well enough so as to be taken for a native. Therefore, I was able to enroll in the University of Puerto Rico. In my junior year, looking to fill my class schedule with an elective class, I decided I would take up a class I could have fun in, so I took up tennis. I was practicing at the courts one day, when in the court next to mine, I couldn't help but notice a flurry of activity. A local campus tennis ace was being given a severe thrashing by a solemn-faced and determined lithe young man. The newcomer

4

wasn't as athletic or as young as his opponent, but made up for his lesser athletic ability, in sheer determination. It was thrilling to watch. Little by little, tenacity won over skill and pretty soon a defeated amateur walked past me, towel over his shoulder, and his tennis racquet poking out of his duffle bag, a picture of dejection. I looked at the departing figure and then happened to look up at the sweat drenched victor, whom I later learned, was Bob, and saw him motion me to play him next. I took him up on it, but in spite of my determination, after about an hour of hard play, the same results ensued. Afterwards, while showering and changing in the locker room, we talked and swapped a little of our life stories and scheduled to meet some time later for drinks at an off campus local bar. There we both proceeded to get smashing drunk and then parted ways. From then on we met again on several occasions and became best buddies, but for some reason, and I couldn't put my finger on it, I had a feeling that he was constantly sizing me up although I didn't know why I felt this way, and I put it down to personal paranoia.

As our relationship progressed, we got to feel more comfortable in each other's presence. Indeed I preferred his company than to any of my contemporary classmates whom appeared now, to my eyes, to be immature when compared to him. We must have seemed a sort of an odd couple when we walked together. He was about 6'2" and had a thin wiry figure, and a Paul Newman physique, having a shade of dirty blond hair, and blue eyes. He was always smiling and outgoing ready to make friends. I on the other hand, was 5'9", had inherited my Mom's cinnamon skin, and dark brown eyes and black hair. As was the popular custom among the college students then, I wore a mustache. I was a little stockier than Bob. I was at that time, broody and introverted and not prone to making friends. I learned, to my surprise that Bob was slightly older than I, being 26 at the time, making him seven years older than me. I had always assumed that he was about the same age as me, and he had certainly looked that young. Because of this age difference, I guess, I started seeing him as a father figure and would confide in him more and more. Not that I didn't have any female figures in my life, but the relationships with the female gender at that time were one-dimensional, shallow, and basically physical. I became Robert's shadow, and looking back now, I don't know how he tolerated me, but tolerate me he did. After a time, he started slipping topics of a political nature into our conversations. I would see him look intently as I expressed my views on this or that, and after a while I tended to try to side step these issues, but one particular day, after we had just lunched at the university cafeteria, his expression became serious and he asked me how I felt about U.S. foreign policies in general, and then drifted to the subject of covert operations in particular. In my infinite wisdom, I replied that in essence it was dirty work, but necessary if we were to maintain the American way of life and its values. I could see in his eyes that the answer was satisfactory to him. As the days passed, I sensed a deepening of our relationship. About two months after this, out of the blue one day, he told me he worked for government intelligence.

"What do you mean?", I asked, thinking he was just joking or plain lying.

"Well, what I mean is that sometimes I do some work for the CIA." he replied slowly and deliberately as he scrutinized my reaction. I was stunned, he seemed serious, but I really didn't believe him. I had assumed, and he had led me to believe, that he was a postgraduate student who was working part-time. I still thought he might be joking, but one look at his eyes told me it could be true. I pursued this line of questioning.

"If you are working for the CIA, why are you telling me this, isn't this supposed to be secret work?"

"Well," he said as he smiled, "it is, but I'm in a situation where I need some help with something, and you're in a unique position to help me."

"Me? Do I look like a spy? Are you crazy? You can't be serious!"

Robert just looked at me with amusement, "You've been reading too many thrillers. In reality, the bulk of our work is just boring everyday research, filing, and just plain old paper shuffling. We're experts at building thick files on just about anything and anyone, and 99% of it never gets read again once it's filed, so get rid of the notion that I have a license to kill and that I travel to exotic countries, and that I walk around with a babe on each arm just yearning to get me into bed with me. All I am basically is a glorified secretary, a compiler of data, most of it as I said, boring."

I could feel him gauging my reaction as he spoke. I was a little confused and didn't know what to think. I had heard that CIA work was boring before, mostly from my primary source of information, spy novels. Perhaps he was telling the truth but my gut feeling told me he was involved in quite a bit more. I was, I have to admit, a bit curious, and just to sound him out I asked, in a disbelieving fashion,

"So you say you have a job for me. Just what is it you would want me to do?"

"Look, I don't want you to feel pressured, and if you decide you don't want to be involved I understand."

Now even more curious, I repeated my question, "What is it you want?"

Seemingly reluctantly he said, "Well, it's really a simple thing, and you happen to be in a perfect position to help me. There's this classmate of yours, actually two classmates, that may have association with communist extremists, and we just want to know if it's true. In other words we need corroboration. "

This kept getting more and more bizarre and surreal. He acted as if he had just asked me to find out what two of my classmates liked to have for lunch. Trying to bring this down to terms I could relate to, I asked the basic question,

"Which two are you talking about?"

"Carlos and Rafael."

I knew the ones he was talking about. They were inseparable and always seemed to be isolated from the class and involved in their own little world. Carlos in particular, always was fond of dressing in Army fatigues or variations of them, and had long hair and a goatee *a la* Che Guevara.

"Oh, yeah, I'll just go up to them and ask them if they're stinking communists. It shouldn't be too hard."

"Don't be facetious, of course you'll need a little training, and if you're willing to help, I can give you some pointers on what to say and do. As I said, it's nothing complicated, and, as an incentive, I can give you a small monetary compensation for your efforts."

Well, as a struggling student, the monetary compensation part struck a chord with me, and was the clincher in convincing me to try it out. Under Robert's direction I soon started associating with Carlos & Rafael. Because of my slight English accent, I had to endure jokes about *el americano* in their midst for several months. Taking directives from Bob, I started expressing anti-American sentiments and dissatisfaction with American ideals and politics. After a long initial period of distrust in which I thought I'd never achieve my goal of gaining their confidence, they started warming up to me. Soon I was slamming American values with the best of them, and after a couple of more encounters, they suddenly invited me to a dorm meeting.

There were about a dozen like-minded individuals there, and apparently, I had been talked about for I was greeted by name and generally accepted, although I did sense some mistrust which as the informal meeting went on, seemed to disappear. The fact that liquor made its presence amongst the guests probably helped my situation. Afterwards, I shared the latest developments with Bob, and he calmly stated that the time had come for an increase in my monthly stipend (which I had grown dependent on), but that I had to assume greater risks. He then produced a wristwatch and explained that in reality it contained a miniature camera, a contraption rigged up by a joint Texas Instruments/Nikon effort. He told me he needed pictures of the group and for that effort my monthly payment would be doubled. With that kind of incentive, I was willing to take the risk. He showed me how to operate the camera, and at the next meeting, I was able to accomplish the task of getting everyone's picture.

How I accomplished this without their noticing I'll never know, for I was sweating profusely, and extremely nervous and at one point was caught pointing the camera, but by this time enough liquor had been consumed to dull the senses, and the individual involved just looked at me and said in Spanish, "What the fuck are you so worried about the time for?" and he laughed and then started talking to one of his other companions and immediately disregarded the incident. I, of course, felt my heart race and thought what I was doing would be apparent to everyone, but I managed to get through the evening and return the camera to Bob the next day who was extremely pleased with the results.

"Well Matt, it's time to move on," he told me, "this lemon has been squeezed as much as it can be squeezed. We've got what we wanted and someone else will baby sit these guys"

After this, he assigned me several other different tasks. All of them sort of menial and like he said before, boring. This was my gradual immersion into the world of the CIA, and I would have remained a bit player if it had not been for one particular incident.

2

In my senior year, Bob came into my dorm room one day and I could tell he was a little excited. Sitting on the bed, he looked at me and said:, "Matt, I need your help. I have to ask you to come with me because I need a fluent translator in Spanish, but we're going to do something a little riskier than usual. Let me tell you, this can serve as a springboard for you if you want to work for us, in a fuller capacity."

"Us? You mean for the CIA? "

"Of course for the CIA!"

I had never thought about being a full time agent but the thought did not repel me.

"Well, I guess I can give this thing a try and we can see where it goes from there. What's it about?"

"You're going to have to trust me on this one. Are you game?"

I was a little apprehensive about going to do an unknown task, but I was bored, and at the time, considered myself immortal, so I replied, "Sure, why not?"

Bob smiled, knowing that I had been hooked, even before I knew it. He waited for me to change and then we went down to his car.

On previous trips, I had seen that Bob wasn't prone to answer any questions unless he wanted to so I didn't ask him anything about our excursion. He would supply me with information when and if I needed to know. After some time driving we arrived at the old San Juan section, rounding the corner of the ancient Plaza de Colon, when suddenly we stopped and a young husky Hispanic, about twenty-eight opened the door and jumped into the car.

Bob kept looking forward and without turning his head, said to me, "This is Nicholas. He's Dominican, and he's going to be helping us on our little project."

We kept riding on in silence. I was slightly uncomfortable, after all, what conversation could I carry on with a stranger, going to who knew where, to do God knew what?

I noticed, to my surprise, that we were heading to the Isla Verde sector and apparently headed toward the airport. My suspicions were confirmed when we turned down the avenue that lead toward the terminal. As we entered the parking area, I couldn't help asking, "Are we taking a plane?"

Breaking his customary silence Bob replied, "Yes we are Matt. We're actually going to the Dominican Republic, and Nicholas here was kind enough as to smooth out our entry through the airport and then help us in our little errand. It's amazing what a few thousand American dollars can buy you."

"Dominican Republic!", I burst out, "Are you out of your mind?"

"I just need you to do some translating for me. "We'll be back this same evening."

"This is going too far. I can't leave the island!"

"Trust me. It will be a short quick hop over there and back."

I was very apprehensive but I was already here and they were ready to go, and deep down, I *did* have a trust in Bob based on our time together. It would have been awkward to make him take me back, so I didn't say anything further. Of course, if I had been told where I was going before I got in the car, I probably wouldn't have come.

Finally, after riding in silence for a while, I blurted out, "What's this all about?"

Bob looked at me with a grim smile and answered, "We've got information from one of our Dominican friends, that a group we had financed to mount an offensive attack against President Trujillo, diverted some of the money and have built up their own personal arsenal and become a military force to themselves. According to our source they are using an abandoned hanger near the airport as a warehouse for all the arms. We've also been told that the place is totally unguarded, and so what we're going to do is relieve them of their little stockpile."

"Wait a minute," I interrupted, "I don't understand something here. Didn't the U.S. back Trujillo's regime while he was in power?"

"Well, that was the *official* policy but secretly he had become a nuisance. Initially he allowed American commerce to flourish on the island with a minimum of intervention on his part, but then it came to the point where he began to stick his finger in every pie and even wanted to dictate how businesses should be run. Not content with that he turned to other South American countries and wanted to influence how *they* were run, so we just got tired of it and one day we let some of his more bitter opponents know exactly where and when he was going to visit his mistress and they ambushed him on the way back and took care of him for us. Then we backed Balaguer as his successor. Our previous friends at first supported him but now after his return to power, they suddenly stopped liking us and started stowing the weapons to stage their own personal coupe. We will now relieve them of said arms, before they can harm themselves or us."

"Hold on there," I said, "You want me to go to the Dominican Republic on a *military* operation? I'm a civilian, remember? Why did you bring me into this, what do I have to do with the situation?"

"Well, Matthew my friend," he said to me, "It's not exactly a military operation, but more of an unofficial foray. Like I said, I need a translator, and since I am not as good as you in *el Español*, I decided to bring you in because in a delicate operation such as tonight's, it is absolutely essential I make my instructions understood, and that I understand what is said back to me."

"So you're telling me this is a covert operation?"

"Like I said, it's unofficial but the Company is aware of what I'm going to do."

"So it's a small operation, how many people are involved?"

"We have three trucks, each with four men. We should be in and out in about thirty minutes."

"What's going to happen? Are you sure I'm going to be safe?"

"Of course you are; I wouldn't take you if it weren't. It sounds dangerous but it's really a very routine task, and you'll be given extra compensation."

"Frankly, it sounds like a lot of bullshit to me."

"Listen," Bob said as he turned to face me, "nothing in life is guaranteed, but if I thought the risk was unacceptable I wouldn't have dreamed of asking you to come. Remember, my life is at risk too, and I don't want to die either." after a pause he added, "So what do you say?"

"O.K." I simply said.

I had my doubts, and I didn't like it, in fact I was furious, but despite my apprehension, I was already here, and I let myself be carried away by the moment. During the flight, I tried to control my growing fear. We continued traveling in silence. We arrived at Santo Domingo at San Isidro airport, a small airfield near a town of the same name on the southern coast, and I disembarked from the unmarked transport plane that we had boarded at the San Juan airport. The trucks were waiting on the tarmac and I got into the one that brought up the rear. Through means of a walkie-talkie I relayed orders from Robert to roll forward. Slowly our little convoy approached a desolate and dark area on the outskirts of the airport. It was a hanger constructed of corrugated zinc and which sat quite a way from the main runways on a patch of deep orange-red clay. Apparently, it was used for light private aircraft. It had an eight-foot chain link fence around it, and I saw that its entrance consisted of two sliding gates that were chained and padlocked. I saw a small twin engine outside, but no indication of life. I informed the driver of the lead truck that Bob had requested the gate's padlock be cut and after that we would enter. Two men jumped out and cut the padlock and proceeded to enter. One of them turned to wave the truck through when all of a sudden I saw a flash against the dark backdrop and our man went down, shot in the back and stunned, but saved because of his Kevlar vest. Suddenly deadly gunfire erupted from the hanger all around us. Everyone panicked and the mission was transformed, from a mildly dangerous, but almost routine excursion, into a deadly trap.

The lead truck suddenly burst into flames. The driver opened the door to exit, but caught a bullet and fell dead next to the vehicle. The three remaining men from that truck used it as a flaming shield for protection. My mouth had gone dry, and I felt a knot in my throat. My heart was beating wildly. After the initial shock, the men from the other trucks returned a fierce barrage of fire, and suddenly everything was quiet. Cautiously, but quickly, three men converged on the hanger and entered, only to appear after a few minutes yelling that it was safe. Bob pulled me by my sleeve as I stared in shock and asked me to tell them that the mission was aborted and that three trucks leave immediately which they did. Bob asked for help and three men jumped out from the remaining truck. I relayed his message that they should quickly move the body of our comrade into the truck, which they did. Then they stripped the body completely on Bob's command. I saw three more bodies, which had been the opposing force. Obviously the cache was not unguarded. The information had been wrong.

After picking up our wounded man and sending off the others back to the truck, Bob proceeded to take out from his backpack three devices with timers. He set them for three minutes. Sweat was dripping down my brow as I watched him. Nicholas seemed petrified. Bob set one of the timed devices near some barrels of aviation fuel that were in a back room which looked as if it served as a type of warehouse. Then he came to the front and set two in the middle of the stacks of crates with arms and munitions, I heard sirens far off in the background. My apprehension grew. Bob just looked at us and yelled,

"We have to get out of here fast. Let's go."

We got into the last truck, and floored it until we were alongside the tarmac. We ran out to the runway towards the transport plane as fast as we could go. Our plane had already turned and was ready to taxi down the runway when headlights from Dominican military trucks appeared around the corner. We were just climbing into the plane when a shout from one of the soldiers on one of the trucks indicated that we had been spotted. At that point, a huge explosion rocked the hanger sending an enormous fireball soaring into the night sky. The lead military truck was ablaze, and I saw in the light of the blaze what seemed to be soldiers jumping out of it. The other two trucks following it, still a little ways from the hanger, came to a screeching halt. As our plane taxied down the runway picking up speed for takeoff, I looked back and saw thick black billowing smoke and an orange glow as debris started falling in slow spirals back to the earth. As we took off another secondary explosion rocked the night. A few seconds later, I looked down on the scene, and it seemed so unreal, so detached from my life. It was hard to believe that just minutes before I had been in the very real danger of losing my life there. My breath was coming in short gasps and I was drenched in sweat. Bob also was looking at the conflagration, the orange reflecting off his face. He sensed I was looking at him and he turned to me and commented with a wry smile,

"A little C-4 goes a long way."

I was so paralyzed with emotions, I couldn't respond. Bob just smiled again and said

"Welcome to the real CIA son."

That little incident had happened over twenty years ago. I remembered being amazed at the distorted story that came out in the press. All that was mentioned was that the hanger had mysteriously caught fire and due to the storage of aircraft fuel, there had been an explosion. According to the news item, no one was hurt and the fire had been put out by local firemen in a matter of hours. The matter of how the fire started was under investigation. No mention of bodies, soldiers, explosives, or of any of the real events of that night. I asked Bob how that had come to be, but he just smiled enigmatically and never gave me a straight answer.

Sometime after this event, I was contacted by Bob asking if I was ready for official full training and after thinking about it I said yes. Arrangements were made and I was sent to Langley going through the process of recruitment as it were, in reverse order. First I had gone on a mission, and then received my training. The fact that my father was in the military and was well known in some Washington circles, and Bob's good word facilitated my being accepted.

Now, Bob had died, not from an outside enemy, but from an enemy within, pancreatic cancer. He had gone through excruciating pain, and I tried to be there for him as much as possible, but it was mental torture to see my friend this way. I came to dread the almost daily trips to the hospital. Mercifully the end came quickly. In accordance with his wishes, he body was cremated and his ashes poured from the outside wall of *El Morro,* a beautiful 16 th century Spanish fort built on the most northern tip of San Juan, the capital of Puerto Rico. I watched silently as the remains of my best friend floated out into the bright blue Caribbean Sea. I watched until I could not see any sight of the ashes and then I stood there until darkness came and I could see no more.

3

ollowing that evening I mechanically followed the proper directives. I was to go to Bob's house for the cleanup. As I turned to
get back to my car, I was intercepted by one of my junior agents.

"Mr. Hines, I think you better get to the beach house as soon
as possible. Something extraordinary has come up."

Arriving at the beach house complex I saw a line of dark
Suburbans parked in the front and several men out on the porch
with their dark sunglasses and casual wear looking for all the world
like bored tourists. As I stepped into the house I perceived a silence and tenseness in the atmosphere. Mark, the agent who had
bought me, beckoned that I should follow him. I went with him and
entered Bob's bedroom. Mark motioned for two agents that were
standing in front of a bedroom linen closet to step aside and they
did so.

"Take a look at this, sir."

With that he dramatically opened the closet door and I peered
inside. I saw what looked like a large number of small yellow ruled
note pads wrapped in bundles and sealed in clear plastic sandwich
bags. Puzzled I asked, "What is this?"

"They're notes"

"Notes? What kind of notes?"

"Apparently Bob made notes of every assignment he's ever been on. They're categorized by date, and have every detail of his work including dates, names, locations, etc."

I looked at him astonished. "You're kidding me!"

"Take a look for yourself"

I reached for a packet and opened it. I recognized Bob's neat handwriting on the yellow sheet immediately. It was dated August 15, 1987. It talked about a case which I recognized, in which he and I had both worked on. A handful of Cuban refugees had reached the Puerto Rico coast in a rubber dinghy and immediately had asked for asylum. During routine interrogation, one of the men, apparently to garner favor with the American officials, had told them that one of their group was in fact, a spy for Fidel Castro. This was verified with another refugee from the group who did so only under threats of deportation, and great reluctance. This is where Bob and I were called in. The two informers had been relocated to Texas along with two more of the group so as not to awaken suspicion, and the other three were left on the island. We monitored the activity of the suspect closely and after a few months paid him a surprise visit at his new abode. After threatening a protest to the INS, Cuban government, and any official agency he could think of, Bob used persuasion techniques and some cash to convince him not to file a complaint, and furthermore, he explained, it would be to his advantage to work for us, ever since, he had provided Cuba with agency-fed misinformation, and had indeed opened a window of information for us on the Cuban government.

THE PRESIDENT'S PAPERS

All this was sensitive information. Yet here it was with specific dates, names, actions taken, locations, etc. I looked at the notes in disbelief. This was against even the most basic rules of the Agency.

"What the hell was the purpose for this?" I asked.

"We don't know sir. We don't believe he sold any of it. We already checked his accounts for undisclosed deposits, and unless he had secret accounts we haven't found, there wasn't anything out of the ordinary. But it's all here beginning with his first year and going on until a month before his death. I guess he was too ill to write by that time."

"I just can't believe it. Why would he do something like this? He never mentioned any of it to me ever."

I flipped through the packets recognizing dates, events, people, everything Bob had ever worked on. This was so odd and bizarre that I was at a loss on how to proceed. Finally I made a determination.

"Here's what we're going to do. I want all of this packed and then we'll have a plane fly this to San Juan and then we'll have a transport fly it over to Langley. Let the guys over there analyze it."

The agent turned to his underlings.

"Ok boys you heard the man."

Immediately the two agents that had been guarding the closet obtained some boxes and started packing them closely with the packets.

Meanwhile, I started to think of what kind of report I was going to write. This was going to be a sticky one. I didn't want to betray my best friend's memory, but then again, I couldn't very well gloss

---

23

over the facts. As I pondered over the report, the guys finished boxing the packets. A Cessna 172 Skyhawk had flown over from the Mayaguez airport with an Agency pilot who was to fly the cargo to the San Juan airport. For all he knew he was probably just moving some obsolete computer equipment.

4

Ruben Irizarry carefully maneuvered his 1998 Grand Marquis through the steep narrow streets of the small coastal town of Arecibo, Puerto Rico. It was a very hot day. He was approaching the plaza. Every town in Puerto Rico had a plaza, and the plaza was the center of activity for every town. The number of people on the sidewalks grew thicker. Portly matrons pulling little children along, some with ice cream or candy in their hands, elderly men walking with a vacant stare and walking steadfastly ahead with a purpose known only to themselves, young curvaceous tan female beauties flaunting themselves, walking a step behind their families as young mustached men gazed lustfully after them leaning against storefront columns. Once in a while, the young men were rewarded with a turn of the head and a smile from the object of their desire. It was a fascinating, never ending parade of sounds, vivid colors, perfume, and activity which made for wonderful people watching. They filled the main street that radiated from the south side of the plaza, and which was the main commercial area of the town, as a myriad of small shops, larger stores, and alley kiosks competed for the attention and money of the passersby. The opposite side of the plaza was occupied by a large Catholic church, (the Catholic churches had monopoly of all the town plazas in Puerto Rico and were present in each and every town). It was to the east side of the church were Ruben was headed, as it was here that all the *carros publicos* (or public cars) congregated. The public car system is a system which, as far as I know, is unique to Puerto Rico. Anyone with a car and a clean driving record can apply for a fixed route that he is willing to service. This route can be from town to town or from town to different sectors of the same town or adjoining *barrios*. A fixed price is established for the route, and the residents alongside the route knew *the* prevailing rate, (usually a modest sum), or if they were traveling to another town or sector they could obtain the rate from the driver. Residents could be seen alongside the roads at any time of the day, waiting for the *publicos* to come along with their distinctive yellow license tags, some with the name of their destination written with decal letters across the top portions of their front windshields. They can be flagged down at any portion of the route, and if the passenger is lucky, there would be only one or two more passengers in the car, but more often than naught, he or she had to squeeze in as the sixth or even seventh passenger in the car. When they arrive at the main street, they are dropped off and then the empty car proceeds to the *publico* depot, which was what Ruben was doing, to take his turn to wait for six or so passengers to fill his car to make the trip in the opposite direction. If a passenger was desperate to leave quickly, he could offer to pay the rate of six passengers making the car, in effect, his own private taxi, but those occasions were rare.

Sometimes, as today, things were very slow, and so the different drivers passed the time by playing checkers or dominos under portable tables set under the luxuriant trees which usually bordered the plazas. A plaza bench would become the seat for one side of the table, and then crates, folding or plastic chairs filled the other sides. The drivers spent many a hour playing, drinking beer, or soda, and eating the various prepared food treats from the cart vendors around the plaza. Usually a cheap radio cassette would be blaring salsa, merengue, bolero, or some other tropical rhythm. Many hours were spent on discussing a wide range of topics including women, sports, world events, politics, (the latter usually avoided because of the heated discussions that ensued), and everything else under the sun. It was a good life.

It was here that Ruben walked to after purchasing a beer and perching himself on the plaza wall he looked on at the activity, listening to the small talk. He was half falling asleep from the effects of the alcohol and heat when suddenly one of the domino players turned suddenly and increased the volume on the radio. Ruben's ears immediately perked up. According to a news bulletin, it seemed that a small plane had crashed into a mountain near the Dos Bocas River, about an hour away, in the central mountain range. The pilot had died, but aside from that there was no detailed information yet. A murmur of voices discussed the event and then everyone settled back and resumed their game. Ruben, on the other hand, jumped from his perch on the wall, and after stating he had remembered some task he had to do, said goodbye to his companions and walked quickly to his car.

Once at the wheel, he immediately started driving to the site of the accident. Arriving upon the scene, his curiosity was piqued by the fact that military police seemed to have taken charge of it. Why would the military be involved? In Ruben's case, this was not a question of mere curiosity. Ruben was a spy. He was born in Matanzas, Cuba, a small town roughly fifty miles east of Habana. He had been an ardent believer in the Cuban revolution, and it's then young charismatic leader, Fidel Castro. He became a loyal Castro supporter and when asked if he would be willing to go to the Dominican Republic, and try to infiltrate into Puerto Rico he jumped at the chance. He was thrilled at the opportunity to serve his country. The trip had been facilitated by a set of false papers and a bribed customs official and it had seemed to Ruben that it had been done so easily. Once in Puerto Rico, he was given a set of orders to establish himself as a *publico* driver as this would give him ample liberty to roam all over the island without suspicion while keeping tabs on anything of note occurring in his assigned territory.

At first, Ruben set out with patriotic zeal to acquire as much information as he could about any situation his supervising contact wanted him to gather at any given moment. As time went on though, he realized that his cover as a driver allowed him to make a real income allowing him to enjoy the conveniences of a capitalistic society, including its luxuries, and even though he wouldn't admit it to himself, as he observed the capitalistic life in Puerto Rico, he had grown slightly disillusioned with the communist ideology, although still remaining marginally faithful to his mission. It was thus that he had found himself to be standing on the river bank, getting as close as he dared to the scene of the accident trying to get a good look as to what was happening.

He peered upstream through a cover of riverside vegetation and saw to his surprise what seemed like a throng of military police guarding the river banks, while another group of military searched among the rocks in the river. A knot of angry looking local police were being kept at bay and they were huddled around their squad cars forced to being simple spectators. Ruben wondered as to what they could be searching for, as the airplane debris was a good distance further upstream from where they were looking. He soon had a partial answer when one of the searchers let out a yell while lifting up a water-drenched plastic bag which seemed to contain some kind of notebook pads so that his companions could see it. Why would this be so important so as to bring this show of military force so quickly? Ruben wanting to get a better look, slid closer to the river bank and without realizing it, placed one foot into the water to maintain his balance. He stood there for a while taking in the scene and analyzing it doing his best to remain undetected. Oblivious to the heat, and the flying insects, he was so absorbed in his task that at first he barely felt the gentle bumping on his leg, but when he became aware of a persistent brushing against his ankle he suddenly jumped back in a reflex action, and looked down to see what had come in contact with him. To his surprise, he saw that it was a plastic wrapped packet identical to the one he had seen one of the military searchers find minutes ago floating in the river current. He immediately crouched down behind the bush and grabbed at the packet and hauled it in. He peered around the bush to see if he had been noticed. Apparently not, everyone was still concentrated on the search, everything seemed as before. He put the packet under his shirt and walked in the same crouching position to the car, got in, and drove off.

5

I was trying to deal with the news and its implications. According to the Sergeant in Charge we had a run of considerable good fortune. One of the two plastic containers in which the memos had been packed had broken on impact spilling its contents into the river. All the packets had been located except one, and he expressed confidence that the last one would be found shortly. The other container was relatively intact. After a fruitless effort to find the final packet the search was extended further downstream.

I was apprehensive, I didn't like loose ends and I wouldn't be able to relax until the last packet was found. I remained on location and paced up and down the river bank scowling at each and every searcher which probably didn't make the situation any more pleasant for them. After a couple of hours, dusk had set and searchlights were brought in and along with them came clouds of mosquitoes which seemed to feast on me as if I were a rare filet mignon. The heat, the bites, the humidity, the darkness, along with the stress, made the situation only slightly better than hell. And still the packet did not show up. After a few more hours, I was ready to personally call it quits for the night. I was a walking zombie. The others would continue the search throughout the night. Another senior agent who had happened to be on leave on the island from Caracas, Venezuela was to help out, and he would take the grave-yard shift. Unfortunately for him, the island had turned out to be the wrong place to be on for his vacation. I took a late shower and crawled into bed about three in the morning. As soon as I closed my eyes I was fast asleep.

I awoke with a start at the strident ring of the hotel phone. I glanced at the cheap digital radio clock on the bedside table. It was 6:35 in the morning. Bleary eyed and irritated, I picked up the phone.

"Mr. Hines?" a female voice queried.

"Yes?"

"I'm calling on behalf of Mr. Gardner, the Director of Intelligence. He is on the island and wants to meet with you this morning."

Instantly the cobwebs in my mind disappeared and I was fully alert. The Director of Intelligence was here on the island? Why had he traveled here? What did he want with me?

"Mr. Hines?"

"Yes, I'm sorry, I wasn't fully awake. When does he want to meet, and for what purpose?"

"I'm afraid that I cannot explain the purpose of the meeting at this time, but he would like to see you at *El Caracol* at 12:00 for lunch. Do you know where that is?"

Apparently, someone had done their homework. Of course I was familiar with the *El Caracol*. It was one of the bar cafes bordering the Guanica Bay, which specialized in serving the freshly caught fish from the bay in different succulent traditional local dishes. It had been a favorite haunt of Bob's, and I had met with him there on many occasions and it quickly became a favorite of mine.

"Yes, I'll be there."

"Thank you."

And that was the end of that conversation.

Around 11:00 I was tying the laces on my reliable Speer boat shoes, and after running a brush through my hair I was ready to go. A half hour later I arrived at *El Caracol* and sat down at one of the small outside tables that offered an unparalleled view overlooking the bay. It was a beautiful warm and breezy day and there was a sprinkling of locals enjoying the fresh seafood & local beer. I ordered a grilled red snapper with onions, french fries, and a *Medalla* beer and settled in to wait. I was absorbed in looking at the small fishing boats anchored in the bay when my thoughts were interrupted by a voice at my back.

"Mr. Hines?"

I rose and turned and saw a young tall agent in a dark suit and dark glasses who looked as if he had stepped straight out of the *Men in Black* movie set. Behind him was Mr. Gardner, the Director of Intelligence. I recognized him mostly from photos and a brief encounter and introduction at a Company gathering several years back. He was about as tall as the agent; I figured about 6' 1''. He was wearing a yellow *guayabera*, a type of dress shirt that was used throughout the Caribbean islands.

He had a flushed red face, as if the exertion of walking in the tropical heat of the day was too much for him. He had a white mane of hair and two eye slits from where one could see a pair of cobalt blue eyes peek out. He and his companion blended in as easily as two clowns at a funeral.

He smiled as he extended his hand and said, "Mr. Hines?"

"One and the same." I answered also smiling as I shook the extended hand. He probably had memorized my face from dossier pictures.

"Nice lunch you got going there", as he sat at my table.

"Can't beat the fish here. You should try the snapper; it's the best in the world."

"Well, Mr. Hines, I'll have to take your word on that, but right now I would like to talk to you on a sort of delicate matter as soon as you finish."

"Oh, I'm already done." I replied as I fished for my wallet.

"Don't bother; your lunch is on me." Motioning to the accompanying agent he gave him the order to take care of the tab, and to me he beckoned, "Come with me please. I'd like to talk to you in my vehicle."

I followed him to the dirt lot in the back of the establishment where another of the favorite of the Company's, a black *Suburban* awaited us. This one was an extended version of the Z71, with dark tinted windows, giving it a rather sinister look. He opened one of the back side doors and motioned me in. I seemed to walk into a small office. There were two captain chair seats facing a small desk complete with laptop computer and a floor bookcase with books on assorted computer programs, books on languages, maps, esoteric types of chemistry, and other Company related reference material. Mr. Gardner took his place at the desk and at the same time the agent hopped into the driver's seat. "You don't mind if we drive around a bit?"

"No, not at all." The vehicle started moving even before I answered.

"Can I call you Matt, Mr. Hines is so formal sounding?"

"Sure." He could call me anything he wanted; after all he authorized my salary.

He fiddled with some dials on an electronic device on his desk. I recognized it as a LADS-2000, a scrambling device that generated sounds that foiled microphones or any other listening apparatus.

"You can never be too careful." he said as he leaned back in his chair.

He seemed to scrutinize me for a long while before finally telling me what was on his mind.

"Matt, do you know who the Babushka lady was?"

Well I was a little confused, and if it was who I thought it was, then I knew all about her.

"Are you talking about the Kennedy assassination?"

"Yes, as you know, in '63 when President Kennedy was assassinated the best recorded evidence we had of the event was the Zapruder film which I'm sure you're familiar with."

"Yes I am."

"Well let me review the events as you may know them. Abraham Zapruder was a local tailor who happened to be at Elm St. in Dallas that day to film the presidential motorcade with his trusty Bell & Howell movie camera as it went by. To get a better look he climbed up on a concrete abutment in Dealey Plaza. When the motorcade came by, he did indeed get the clear view he wanted, and as he filmed, the assassination occurred, capturing on film, the clearest record of the event that we have today. As much publicity as was given to this by the press, there was a an better witness to the event that was never discussed in the press much. On Zapruder's film she's seen filming the motorcade from the opposite side, and she had a clearer view of the events, and more importantly, she filmed the side of the street where the majority of conspiracy theories place other possible assassins. If you look at these," he said as he handed me some pictures, "You'll see the women who is referred to as the Babushka lady. As you probably know, she was given that moniker because of the kerchief she is wearing in the style of the babushka worn by the Russian female peasants. As you can imagine, in the days after the assassination, the Zapruder film was analyzed and it became painfully obvious that she was the best witness and so the media hunt for the Babushka lady was on. In 1970, a certain woman, came out and pronounced herself the Babushka lady, and said that her film had been confiscated after the incident by FBI agents and she never saw it again. That's the official story."

"And, I suppose you're going to tell me there's another story."

He sat back with a smile on his face, while tapping a pencil across the palm of his hand. He looked like the Chestshire cat from Alice in Wonderland.

"Yes indeed, there is another story. Have you ever wondered why *every* other person in that plaza that day has been identified by name, address, occupation, and every detail imaginable, *except* for the most important witness, the Babushka lady?

"The thought has crossed my mind."

"That's because we knew who she was and we wanted to hide her. One of the FBI's informants was glad to assume the identity of the Babushka lady for a little gift of fifty grand that we paid her to play the role. At the time, she was a dancer, and sometimes picked up a little cash by being a paid informant for the FBI, and was only too glad to get the substantial payday. She was told to spend the money discreetly. One of our people coached her on what her story would be for the press. Of course, they made the mistake of not coaching her appropriately especially on the all-important little details. When she was asked at a press conference what type of camera she was using she didn't know what the answer was supposed to be and she panicked. She recalled an ad for a Yashica Super 8 she had seen in a magazine and mentioned that as the camera she had used. That seemed like a smart move, except for the fact that the particular model of camera she mentioned wasn't even commercially available at the time of the assassination. The fix we came up with, was to add a "friend" that worked with Yashica who had let her borrow a prototype, which I thought was a ludicrous story, but the American public, God bless them, are like a giant flock of sheep. Whatever you told them at that time, they believed, especially if they saw it in print. The prevailing attitude of the day was 'If it was in print it must have be true'. Or at least that's the way they thought in those days, but since then, as you know, modern investigative reporters have opened up the eyes of the public, and now everyone's become slightly distrustful of everything governmental or official, as well they should be. But the informant's story held and we were all glad for that. We felt like the magician who does a trick and thinks to himself, 'Surely they noticed how I did that', but the audience claps wildly and is duly impressed and completely fooled."

He stopped there to build suspense. There was a self-evident question in the story and I knew that he wanted me to ask it, so I complied.

"So why did you want to hide the identity of the real Babushka lady?"

"The real lady, as you put it, was Mila Asimov, a low level Russian spy. We knew of her, and had allowed her to keep operating in the U.S. on purpose. We wanted to analyze how she communicated with her network, and to try to identify who her contacts were. You can imagine our surprise when we realized she was on the film. We hadn't even filled in the FBI about her presence. It would have been extremely embarrassing to us, to say the least, if the facts had come out. She could have just as easily could have been one of the assassins. The agency went into panic mode and the word went out to have her picked up regardless of the repercussions. We had to come up with a body for the woman in the film so we came up with our occasional informer turned Babushka lady. Mr. Hoover, the FBI director at that time, knew that we had some kind of involvement in the situation but didn't know exactly what, and he didn't have any proof of anything so he had to stay put, albeit in a smoking rage. The thing is that we caught Mila at one of her drop off points a day later, and we struck pay dirt, she had just passed on the film. She cracked under interrogation and divulged that she had passed it on to a Russian KGB agent who had gone immediately to Cuba and who was to forward it to his superiors.

This is where your friend Robert comes in. His mentor in the service was a certain agent you may of heard of, William Baker."

He looked at me with a questioning look.

"Bob had mentioned him to me in a general way, and some things they had done together but not with any great detail. I am aware at least in name, of who he was."

"Well at that time, Will had cultivated contacts in Cuba, and knew of the traveling Russian KGB agent, so we advised him of the situation and of the need to obtain the film. We wanted to contain the information so we advised him that everyone else should be left out of the loop, he acceded since he had developed Spanish contacts on the island that he could work with.

He rapidly identified the agent as Vasiliy Havlik through an immigration contact he had, and through the same he ascertained that he was staying at the *Hotel Nacional* in Habana. He was receiving the five star treatment. That night, while he was out with a *jinetera*, (one of the hundreds of young girls who roam the streets of Habana in search of tourists who will buy them gifts such as dresses, perfumes, a meal at a restaurant, or anything of value, in exchange of company and/or sex), William had the hotel concierge make him a key to the agent's room and in the same night installed a miniature camera, nothing elaborate you understand, but enough for his purposes. When Vasiliy returned with his little tart, and was occupied with her, three loud raps were heard at the door. Vasiliy sat up erect in the bed, like a frightened hamster. Three more load raps were heard and Vasily immediately turned in direction of the bathroom then thought better of it, and after slipping a Russian PSS silent pistol into the back of his wrap-around towel he turned his attention to the disturbance at the door. He stood at the threshold and asked "Who is it?" in a loud voice. A timid voice had replied in Spanish "I'm sorry sir; I did not mean to disturb you." Keeping a grip, behind his back, on the PSS, he slowly opened the door to find a young red-faced Cuban hammering a nail to add a newly framed picture to the already existing ones along the hallway. "I'm sorry sir", he repeated, "I will do this in the morning, I thought this section of rooms was empty." Vasiliy, a little suspicious watched the young man with the picture under his arm walk away until he disappeared down the hall-way then he looked around suspiciously, and rationalized that per-haps the worker's story could be true as this room had indeed been allocated in a special section of the hotel just for him and the worker was possibly unaware of this room being occupied, also there was the allure of the young girl waiting for him. He returned and went into the bathroom, and this time took a shaving cream canister from the shelf near the sink and unscrewed the false bottom and verified the film was still there. Then he decided to put it in the medicine cabinet for better safekeeping. Just then, the *jinetera* started beckoning to him from the bedroom and he immediately turned his attention else-where. Later that night, drinks were ordered, and William made sure that chloral hydrate was part of the mixed cocktails. The powerful hypnotic had its effect and within an hour, both the Russian and the young girl were fast asleep in each other's arms. After a little more surveillance from the fish eye lens of the mini-camera he had installed in the room's ceiling fan, the door silently opened and a figure entered, went into the bathroom, took out the canister from the medicine cabinet and after unscrewing the bottom, took out the film and substituted it with a blank film. He then slipped out and silently closed the door behind him.

Of course, when the KGB developed the film and discovered the film was blank they were furious. There were serious repercussions.

Vasily's actions that night were fully investigated and he was found in the same hotel room several days later, dead of an "accidental" drug overdose. What was left of Mila was discovered at the bottom of a ravine in the Tennessee Mountains still in her car. The scene was ruled accidental and the body remained unidentified, but the prints were a match for records we had, which of course had been tagged by the Company and the records disappeared as soon as the match was made. As for the film, we have it, and of course, the information on it is classified."

I was flabbergasted by the revelation of the existence of the film, and how we had come to be in possession of it. Equally disturbing was the fact that I was being told all this information without needing to know about it and I wanted to know why this was so. So the next question was obvious.

"Why am I being told all this?"

"Because, back in 1984 we had a meeting to review the developments in regard to the analysis of the film at which Bob and some of our other key people were present, and as you know, the plane that went down recently had your friend's memoirs. We recovered as you know, all the packets except one," He paused here for dramatic effect, "the one that is missing happens to be the one detailing Bob's exploits at the Cuban hotel and the extraction of the film. So as you see, it's extremely important that we recover it. The release of the information it contains would be extremely prejudicial to our diplomatic standings with several foreign countries and it could create political and social havoc here in the states. It's essential we get it back at any cost."

So *that* was the reason of this whole elaborate meeting. It all clicked into place now. But I still couldn't see what he expected of me. Did he think I had a little magic wand that I could wave and make everything O.K.? The chances of finding that packet were dwindling. Several hundred men had searched already for more than fourteen hours. Only if one of the searchers had hidden it for personal gain, might we have a small chance of finding out about it and take steps to get it back. Already my mind went into high gear. An exhaustive background check would have to be initiated on each and every one of the hundreds of searchers. This was going to take a lot of time and effort. I communicated these concerns to Mr. Gardner.

"As I said, whatever it takes. You will have free rein on expenses, as long as an accounting is provided to me. We will try to provide you with any personnel and resources you may need. You are free to use any means necessary to obtain information leading to the recovery of the packet. Do you have any questions?"

Of course, I was in total shock, and my brain was paralyzed, so I just said "Not at the moment."

"Good, if you think of anything or need anything call this number." He underlined a number on an ad for a bar on a book of matches. "That's *our* number camouflaged as the ad, so make sure you don't lose those matches."

Standing up, he offered his hand saying "Good luck.", and I shook it saying I would do my best.

Then I was left standing by the side of the bay watching the black Suburban disappear and asking myself, 'How the hell did I get into this mess?'

6

Ruben, the Cuban spy, had informed his superiors of the accident and what he witnessed. To not do so would have awakened suspicions. He had reported the circumstances of the accident, the type of aircraft involved, the U.S. military involvement, what they were looking for, in other words, everything except for the fact that he had found one of the packets and that it was in his possession. Instinctively, he knew that what he had was valuable and he only had to figure out who it was valuable to, and then contact that person or organization, let him or them know what he had, and then settle on a price, all without losing his skin. This would be a very delicate operation he concluded, and it would require a very fine touch. He didn't even know where to begin. The first thing, he decided, was to see exactly what he had, so he reached into the drawer were he kept the packet and with a razor he carefully cut open the sealing tape and then withdrew the notepad within and started reading.

As he read his breathing came faster and faster, and he felt a cold sweat coming on. He was fascinated and could not put the notes down. After some time, he had finished and just sat at his chair in shock. This was gold! It was explosive! He could think of several agencies and countries who would be very interested in buying this material, including the Soviet Union, Cuba, The FBI, the CIA, and even U.S. media. His head was spinning. Who would pay the most, and with the least difficulty? How could he make the proper contacts? 'Let's take it one step at a time,' he told himself. Who would pay the most? Offhand; and thinking logically, it would be the people most embarrassed by the information and that would be, by far, the CIA. In contacting any one party first, he would automatically be alienating any other possible clients, so he probably only had one shot at this, and he had to think this through carefully. Even with their corrupt officials the communist countries probably couldn't come up with the kind of cash that the American counterparts could. And, as he had speculated before, the Americans would probably be more prone to want to stop the embarrassing information from leaking out. Now, the problem would be how to feed the lion without having the lion tear your head torn off. This was a complicated matter.

As he drove his fares that afternoon, (he had decided to keep working so as not to arouse suspicions), he thought of Andres Segarra. This was the only possible CIA operative that Ruben knew on sight and that he could have personal contact with. Andres ran an ice cream shop on the perimeter of the town plaza. Ruben had heard rumors from several people that had traveled in his *carro publico* stating that they thought Andres was working with the CIA, but he had not communicated this information to his controller because he never did have any hard facts to pass on. Also, in the back of his mind he had always kept the thought of keeping the rumor secret just in case the possibility of an opportunity such as this would materialize. So far, all he had heard was merely gossip. Now it was time to put the gossip to the test.

The next morning as Andres Segarra opened the thick padlock on the iron grating at the front of his store and pushed open the door to his ice cream shop, he spied an envelope lying on the floor. Stooping to pick it up he noticed that it had no writing on it. Intrigued, he opened it and unfolded a note written in Spanish which read:

Dear Friend,

Although I am a rival of yours, I have come across some information which would be of utmost interest to your Company and I am willing to trade it in exchange for monetary consideration. If you are willing to hear more about my proposition please leave a vertical chalk mark on the antique lamppost on the northwest corner of the plaza.

Sincerely,
Cachorro

Needless to say, Andres was startled by the missive. He had taken great pains to cover his tracks and thought he had been successful. Now someone apparently knew of his secret activities. Cachorro was the Spanish word for cub, so that was obviously a false name. Upon reflecting, he decided that the note had originated with someone within the intelligence community, someone who was not above dipping his hand in the cookie jar for personal gain. The thought that he had been observed, without he himself observing anyone, frightened him a little. Andres' heart fluttered. This was a dangerous game. What should he do? After thinking about it for a while, he decided to contact me. He wrote out a missive detailing all that had happened and attached it the original note that he had received. He made this into a small bundle and ran a strip of masking tape across it. He went outside, crossed over to the plaza and sat on a bench directly across from his shop. Having the note in his palm, he bought both hands to the bench edge, slid the his palms under it and made a motion as if he were stretching, at the same affixing the note with pressure, under the bench. He bent his head between his legs and ascertained with his fingers that the note was well attached, and then he raised his arms over his head and stretched again. To a casual observer it looked as if Andres had crossed to the plaza to take in the morning sun before opening shop, and was stretching and reluctantly willing himself to start working. After some minutes, he rose and went back into the store, and dug up a hand-made sign from behind the counter. It said 'Lo sentimos, helado de coco no disponible temporeramente', which translated meant, 'We're sorry, but coconut ice cream is temporarily unavailable.' This he taped to the window of his shop. Later that day, Emilio saw the sign on his daily recon, parked his car on one of the side streets, and with *El Nuevo Dia*, (the local daily paper) under his arm, ambled to the bench and sat down to read. After about ten minutes, he leaned to scratch his leg, slid his hand under the bench and retrieved the note. He hid the note in the paper and returned to the car where he opened it. After reading it, he realized it was very important, and after calling me, bought it over the very same day.

Upon reading it, I immediately realized that I had probably reeled in the long shot. The note could be referring to something else, or it could be a practical joke, but it was more than likely someone had found the packet somehow, and was trying to sell it. I surmised, just as Andres had, that the person was from the intelligence community. It was probably someone with low ranking because if his greediness were discovered he would probably be executed and he was too dumb to realize that. Also, in all likelihood, the full import of the information he had hadn't dawned on him. It was enough to change history. Making these assumptions, I had to decide on how to best play this. We would have to set up a meeting, add a surveillance team, verify that we were talking about the packet, and then identify who was involved. Future action depended on what we obtained. Instructions were given to Andres to put up the mark on the lamppost and we anxiously awaited further developments.

Two days later, Andres received a letter in the mail. It came inside one of his credit card bill statements. Apparently his mail had been intercepted, the bill opened, the note inserted and then the envelope had been crudely resealed. I would have everything dusted for prints but wasn't expecting positive results, and indeed, a few days later the results arrived and were as expected, negative. Moreover, a DNA analysis for saliva had the same result, so we weren't dealing with a complete amateur. The note mentioned that Andres should be at the *Cruz del Vigia* observation deck at 1 pm the following Tuesday to receive more information.

The *Cruz del Vigia* was a 100 foot high monument tower in the shape of a cross with observation decks for visitors which overlooked the city of Ponce, the second largest city on the island of Puerto Rico. Located on the central southern coast, the structure provided a breathtaking view to the visitors, of the city and the Caribbean Sea beyond. It originally had been a lookout spot, a viewing point of approaching ships to determine if they were friend or foe. The site was chosen because it was the highest mountain near the sea. A wooden pole with a cross beam to stand on had been erected at the site so that a better view could be obtained. Then later, the modern monument was built. The original wooden cross had stood in front of it, but was partially destroyed by Hurricane George in 1998. The remnant of the original wooden lookout cross was still on display here. It was a popular spot for lovers and tourists.

Andres would have to expose himself as a CIA contact, which was a risk that was unpopular with him, but one we had to take in view of our need to obtain the information we wanted. He would have to set up a meeting and flush whoever had the packet into the open where he could be identified. Going on the assumption that the finder of the memo was operating solo, we concluded he probably didn't have any backup. I would have a little welcome committee set up accordingly to wait for him. He was an unknown entity, and it was too risky to have an unknown entity with explosive information running around. If he was a loner, he would have to be erased permanently.

7

A ndres looked out at the view of Ponce from *La Torre del Vigia*. It was as beautiful and impressive as he remembered it. He could see the whole city displayed before him. He could also see the tiny *Caja de Muertos,* (Coffin Island), which far out in the distance, seemingly looked as it was floating in the Caribbean Sea. It was a gorgeous sunny day. The weather was great, although some clouds were gathering signaling perhaps a chance of rain later on in the day. Standing at one of the observation windows, he looked down at a *piraguero* in the parking lot far below. The *piragueros* were vendors pushing colorful, hand painted carts mounted on a pair of wagon wheels, and as individual as each owner. They carried a block of ice and dozens of brightly colored syrups in bottles, (usually cleaned-out discarded rum bottles), and upon request, they would fill a paper cone with shaved ice, and then poured on top any of the flavored syrups, or combination of them, making a refreshing and flavorful treat for children and adults alike. They were an integral part of the puertorrican landscape, only this particular *piraguero* was Enrique one of the office crew who was poised with a Taurus M850 pistol with silencer ready to eliminate his target if needed, although this was just an emergency backup which hopefully would not be needed.

There were two inconspicuous cars at the scene. One was at the far side of the parking lot and had a female and male agent pair posing as a young couple. The female was Carrie, an expert in photography prepared with a Canon EOS digital camera which she was still resentful of, because she had learned photography on film cameras and still considered that they had the advantage of superior detail of image although she had finally had to give in to the advance of technology. As a backup she also had a Sony MiniDV video recorder she used because of its compact size. They would be the in lead car ready to become mobile and follow our seller if needed, there was a second car further down the road, and I was in a third car, in contact with the main team through video feed from Carrie, and through radio. I was stationed two miles down the most probable route the subject would use and we would form a team running a loose tail on our target. If needed, a company chopper was at our beck and call. Everything was in place. The wait began.

Andres was a very patient man, something that stood him in good stead in this line of work. He glanced at his watch and saw that there was only ten more minutes to go until contact time. He stomach tightened in anticipation. Would the contact come early? After ten minutes had passed the answer was obviously not. After another twenty minutes, Andres concluded this would probably be a no show. He waited another twenty minutes, and wondered if he should call it quits. I made the decision easy for him by calling him on his cell, which he had been instructed not to use for fear of scaring off the target, and told him that indeed, we would be calling it off. If the mystery man hadn't shown up by now, it was highly unlikely he would show. With great reluctance Andres started down the stairs to ground level. Just in case we were being watched, everyone was to leave independently, at predetermined intervals, and we would reconvene later on.

As Andres opened the door and stepped outside he saw a young boy of about fifteen approach him on bicycle and call out to him *"Senor! Senor! Me dijeron que le entregara esta nota."* What the boy was saying, as he waved an envelope at Andres, was that he had been instructed to make delivery of the envelope he held in his hand to him. When Andres asked about the note, the boy told him it was supposed to be from Andres' girlfriend. Upon further questioning, the boy further revealed that a man had approached from the side of the road as he was riding by and called for him to stop. Curious, but slightly frightened, the boy had done so, figuring that it he didn't like the situation he could take off at an instant's notice. The man had kept a safe distance away and explained that he needed a favor. His sister had met his best friend and they were to go on a date today, but his sister had decided she no longer wanted any further involvement with him. He didn't want his best friend to know what had happened and so he had written him a letter pretending it was from his sister, making up an excuse for not showing up. The man had told him that if he delivered the letter he would be given twenty dollars. He accepted and the stranger had advised the boy that he would be watching him to make sure it was delivered. The boy had been given an exact description of Andres down to the gold skull ring he was wearing, and was on the verge of going up the observation floor to find him, when he had seen Andres coming out the main entrance. Andres said *"Espera!"* and handed him another twenty, and opened the envelope. Inside was a copy of the title and date page from the missing packet, and nothing else.

After being appraised by Andres about the situation, we detained and questioned the boy, and searched the spot where he had met up with our stranger. We agreed to meet the next day for a debriefing. The only things obtained from the spot search were shoe prints. The shoes were a 91/2 walking shoe which later was identified as a Thom McAnn shoe sold at K-Mart shoe stores in the thousands so they weren't unique, to say the least. He had apparently parked in between two school buses and walked to the site where he had encountered the young boy so that his tire prints did not show on the asphalt. Any unique traces were obliterated by the dozens of children returning to both buses. The description we got from the young boy was that of a Latino man who seemed to be in his late thirties, about 5'7", with a black mustache. He had a cap on which covered most of his hair, and mirrored sunglasses. He had been dressed in a blue jumpsuit which looked like a mechanic's but close questioning of the boy revealed he not seen a name tag or company logo. The description was too vague; it could fit almost any young male on the island. Except for the fact that we had confirmed that this man indeed had the material we were looking for, and that he had shown he was a little more clever than we thought, we were effectively back to square one.

8

This was a real headache. We had definitely ascertained that someone had obtained the missing information, only God knew how, and was running around with it probably without fully realizing the explosive potential of the material he had. If he tried contacting any other parties which he thought would be interested in it we would hear about it, but I was hoping he was at least smart enough to try his options one at a time. The morning after the tower fiasco, I entered my home office and there was a message on my secure line. It was short and to the point. It was a male voice, which sounded vaguely familiar, telling me to call a number I didn't recognize. I dialed and was shocked to hear Mr. Gardner. I thought he would be using aides, junior agents, or at least his secretary to contact us lower level folk.

"Good morning, Matt. This is Gardner. How are you this morning?"

"Fine"

"I was briefly told about what happened in Ponce yesterday, do you care to fill me in?"

I gave him a synopsis of everything that had transpired.

"This is bad, really, really bad. It's essential that we get that information back."

"I have all my men working their contacts, and I'm personally overseeing everything and making sure that we're doing everything we can."

"I'm going to put my trust in you and if you need any more resources, you just call my office at any time and if I'm not in, ask for Peter Rogers. I'll give instructions to him so that you'll get anything you need."

"Thank you."

"I'll call again tomorrow to see if there's any progress."

"Yes sir, I'll keep working at it."

"You do that. I'll keep in touch."

After he hung up, I thought of how lucky I was that I hadn't been forced to accept outside help, and that just made me more determined to come up with results. I don't take kindly to help being forced on me. I brewed myself some coffee and sat down to think over my next course of action. I called all available agents for a meeting the next day.

The next morning, I had eighteen people talking, drinking coffee, munching on bagels, and milling about in bathing suits, shorts, sunglasses, and other beach apparel. In order not to attract attention, they had arrived posing as a bunch of eco- tourists on a group tour bus and a big show had been made of verifying passes at the gate. They were all enjoying themselves to the max. I circulated amongst them handing out greetings, handshakes, and enthusiastic pats on the back. It looked like an early morning cocktail party. I was just about to go to a small podium we had at one end of the room, when I saw *her* come in. Gina spotted me at about the same time and we locked eyes for several seconds. Everything; sound, people, my surroundings, disappeared as we stared at each other, and then just as suddenly, the spell was broken and she and I returned to simulated normalcy. I had been dreading seeing her, though, secretly I longed desperately for it to happen. How was that for irony? After a few seconds, we both reacted to our surroundings and kept on walking and appeared to be unaffected by each other's presence.

I called for everyone to gather around and for the next three hours we hammered out a plan of action based mainly on increased surveillance, and leaning on all contacts for more information, and an offer of a substantial monetary compensation for any lead that panned out. In reality, we were in the dark. It was the proverbial throw anything at the wall and see if anything sticks approach. Success or failure of the mission would hinge on luck, circumstance, or a mistake on the seller's side. Basically, all I could do was wait and hope for the best. After the discussion of a plan of action, I announced that there would be an outside barbecue before we left and everyone started talking and slowly drifting outside. Several of my colleagues came over and hashed over several ideas with me and then we drifted into general shop talk. After a while, one of the guys said, "I don't know about you guys but I'm hungry. Let's take a crack at those ribs out back!" The group smiled and then also started to go out back. "I'll be right with you guys." I turned to put away some of the potentially sensitive paperwork that was lying on the podium when I looked up and there she was. She was dressed in light cotton, candy cane striped, white and red blouse and powder blue hip-hugging shorts that showed off the curve of her hips. She was leaning against the door frame with a drink in her hands. I approached her from behind and spoke to her, slightly startling her.

"So what's your plan? Were you just going to avoid talking to me altogether, just ignore my existence?"

She turned and looked at me. It was all I could do to restrain myself from rushing over and hug her tightly in my arms but there was a real, but invisible barrier around her.

"Hello Matt," she replied softly with a sad smile, "It's been some time."

"Yes it has," I replied.

I just looked at her, drinking in her image and savoring it. After a couple of seconds of uncomfortable silence she asked, as she looked steadily at me.

"Cat got your tongue?"

"I'm sorry; it's just that you look so incredibly beautiful. You bring back so many memories."

The screen door burst open at that moment and Chuck, one of the field agents, burst in. Looking at us, and sensing the intimacy of the situation, he clumsily said, "Just came to tell you Boss, that the hot dogs, and burgers are ready." and then he sheepishly backed out and let the door bang shut. We turned our attention back to each other.

"No calls?"

"I didn't know how you were going to take it. I didn't want to cause you any aggravation."

"I'm OK."

We both knew she wasn't. We both knew *I* wasn't. We were far from OK. We were hurting, and hurting a lot. We needed each other desperately, and we were just too stupid to say it. I thought back to what had happened and how stupid I had acted.

9

Once in a while, I would spend several weeks at the main San Juan office to coordinate different assignments and supervise what was going on in our territory. After these stays I would return to my Guanica hideaway. About a year ago, Gina had been transferred to my office from Atlanta. I had spotted her as soon as I walked into work that day. I opened the door, and there she was a vision, the carnal personification of my dream girl. She took my breath away. I was wondering if I had walked into another dimension. Why was this beauty, this sublime work of human form in my office? She looked up at me with wide startled eyes when I came in, and I felt transported to another dimension. Manny came over as I stood as if petrified by the front door.

"Hi, boss. How's it going?"

"Fine." I managed to blurt out.

"We have a new addition from Atlanta. They called yesterday about her, but you were in the field. Her name is Gina Villegas. She's going to be here on a permanent placement basis. What a piece, huh?"

I just gave him a dry look, and answered, "Send her to my office in five minutes."

Once in my office, I threw my briefcase on my desk, sat down, and tried to compose myself.

My breathing rate had just about normalized, when there was a knock on the door. It was her.

She peered around the door and said,

"Manny said you wanted to see me."

"Yes, sit down."

She took a seat in front of me.

"I like to meet all our personnel. I understand you're going to be with us on a permanent basis?"

"Yes sir, I was based in Atlanta but I decided to move to Puerto Rico because of personal reasons."

"That's quite a move."

"Well actually, I have an aunt who lives here, and she offered to take me in until I found my own place."

"I see. Well we certainly need the help. We'll show you the ropes, and pretty soon I'm sure, you won't be missing Atlanta." I said clasping my hands and involuntarily leaning forward. She responded by beaming a wide smile and saying, "Thank you sir."

"OK then, let's see about getting you a desk."

I called Yvette, our office coordinator, and had her taken to Ana's desk, a colleague who had been transferred out to Seattle. "After lunch we'll run through some of what we're working on, and how you'll fit in, but for now just settle in and put your things away and look around if you want to, Yvette can give you a tour." After further good byes she left and I tried to concentrate on my work, but all I kept thinking of was her. I next saw her at lunch. She was looking at the food in the cafeteria with what looked like a trace of disdain. I approached her.

"The selection isn't that great, huh?

She seemed a little startled and then replied with a smile.

"It seems my school cafeteria was a step above this one."

It was my turn to smile.

"Well, since this is your first day, I'll tell you what. I'll treat you to lunch."

"Can we do that?"

"I'm the boss, so I'd say yes."

With that I took her to my nearby favorite place "El Patio de Sam", a casual food restaurant which specialized in a mix of local and American style food.

"What's good?" she asked.

"Well if you want something light you can try the 'Antojitos' platter. It's a sampler of all the local favorite snack foods."

"Sounds good. I think I'll go with your expert advice."

"We don't drink during working hours, but since this is your first day, we can bend the rule for once. What'll you have?"

She seemed to blush a little, but answered "How about a piña colada?" "Two piña coladas it is."

An hour later, I had learned that she was born in a small town, Plant City, Florida, and after being raised there she went to study at the University of Georgia, in Athens, Georgia, to, as she put it, 'get far away from her family'. "Not they weren't loving, just that sometimes the loving was a wee bit much."

I smiled, "I can empathize with you completely."

She in turn, listened to my story of being born in New York, raised in Freehold, also a small town, in New Jersey, and then as a teen moving to Puerto Rico when my parents moved. I gave her a short recap of my studies and recruitment by the company and my work. "And," I finished, "Here I am."

We finished, got up, and returned to work strolling down Calle Sol enjoying the warm sun.

During the weeks and months that followed we took other, ever more frequent and longer lunches. As one of the participants in the ever more intimate relationship, I was self-delusional. I thought we were sly, and that no one noticed our growing closer. That's why it caught me by surprise, when one morning Emilio casually said, "Looks like somebody got bit by the love bug." I looked at him astonished and realized I hadn't been as discreet as I had thought and decided we had to be more careful about our relationship, but before that could happen I had to know where we stood. Later that day, at lunch, I led into the big question, "Gina, we've been spending a lot of time together lately." Smiling, she replied, "Yes we have." I looked directly into her eyes and asked, "Do you have feelings for me?" I guess I caught her by surprise. She visibly blushed and lowered her head and then answered in a small voice, "Yes". I reached over and clasped her hand in mine.

"I've loved you since the first time I ever saw you."

"I feel the same way, and it seems amazing to me that you would feel the same way."

I leaned over and gave her a tender kiss, then realizing I was in public I turned to see if anyone from the office was around.

She smiled and said, "Are we caught? Are you that afraid?"

I smiled back, "I have to protect my job."

Still smiling she asked "So that's how it's going to be, we're going to have to hide to kiss?"

I smiled back, "you know that I have to protect myself and I'm also protecting you, I really love you, but until I can figure something out, we have to be cautious."

I embraced her, and afterward we walked back to the office holding hands briefly at times, as giddy as two high school kids afraid to be found out. Before we entered I made plans to pick her up at her apartment for a movie that night. I picked her up at her apartment as planned. We went to a theater in another nearby town, hoping to not be seen. After the movie we went back to her apartment. As soon as the door closed she turned, gave me an ardent kiss and nature took its course. The next morning we felt as if we were on cloud nine, and we almost arrived late for work. For the next couple of months, whenever I was in the San Juan office we would go out, being as discreet as possible, and whenever I was in Guanica, she would try to come down to visit, and we tried to keep everything as light as possible.

During this time period there was a Company junket to Mexico. We were both looking forward to the trip, but with just a couple of days to go, Gina received the news that her favorite aunt had passed away. I was willing to suspend the Mexico trip to accompany her but she said,

"There's no reason for you to suspend the trip. All the family is going to be together and we're going to spend a few days there, the whole bunch. We're going to be reminiscing about family memories and you'll just be as bored as hell. Besides, you know that you're in charge of some of the entertainment, so you have to be there. I'll tell you what, you go, and I'll meet you there after a couple of days." I was a little reluctant to go under those circumstances, but she was right, so with misgivings, I accepted the arrangement.

I felt a lot lonelier at the party than I thought I was going to be. It was incredible that I could be surrounded by so many friends and colleagues and still feel so lonely. I guess I had become more dependent emotionally on Gina than I had realized. I started taking trips to the free bar to make up for it. Somewhere after the fifth drink, Stacy, a procurement officer, suddenly was there at my side, matching me drink for drink, and joke for joke. The next thing I knew, I was waking up with the sound of knocking on my door, and a splitting headache. I got up on an elbow and looked at the clock. It was 8:15am. There was another knock at the door, and then I heard my name called. It was Gina! At that same precise moment, I felt movement at my side, looked over to my left, and saw Stacy wrapped in a blanket, going to the door and opening it. The look of hurt on Gina's face was something I never want to see on anybody's face ever again. She just turned and quietly walked away.

I called out to her, but she just kept walking. I couldn't very well chase after her in my underwear so I ran to put on some pants.

"I'm sorry," Stacy said, "I didn't know who it was."

"It's not your fault." I said hurriedly as I rushed out slamming the door. I rushed out, but it was too late. She was gone.

I called her and left long rambling explanations of what had happened at her home phone and on her cell, but never got a return call. I knew there wasn't any real, valid, explanation for what had happened. I took the first flight I could get back. Again, Gina beat me. She had managed to get on a military flight that had left almost immediately after she had walked out. When I got to the Guanica house I was renting and sharing with her at the time, she was long gone, along with her personal items and a short and simple note that was right to the point and which read:

Do not contact me ever again.

Gina.

The former was going to be impossible since we worked together. I tried to leave yet another explanation on her cell phone but to no avail. I decided that to avoid conflict, I would assign her as far as I could from me and try to contact her after some time had passed. That had been some five months ago, and she had not attempted to call me in all that time, and that's why I was pleasantly surprised when she addressed me.

"I noticed you set me up to operate in San Juan."

That wasn't a statement. It was an accusation. San Juan was in the extreme central north part of the island. It was as far away from Guanica as I could assign her. She thought I had assigned her there on purpose, and she was right. I wanted to get her as far away from me as I could, and then not seeing her so frequently, I could slowly stop obsessing about her and if she never wanted to see me again she could have that option. We just looked at each other and she sensed she that I was embarrassed and ashamed and yet she hesitated to speak.

"Gina" I began, I could barely speak, "I'm sorry".

Tears began to well in her eyes.

"I didn't come up here for an explanation, besides, words are so easy to say and in the end, they don't mean a thing."

"I really do mean them though. You don't know the agony this situation has put me through."

"I just keep asking myself one question, why?"

I had asked myself that same question may times before.

"It was something very, very, stupid. I was acting like a foolish teenager. I realize I'm too old to be foolish now. She was there, we worked a lot together, she stroked my ego, and then that night we got drunk with the guys, I know you won't believe me, but I was drinking only because I missed you, and I don't even remember what happened, and, well, you know the rest. It was a stupid thing, I don't even like her. You're the only woman I've ever felt real love for."

She looked into my eyes and read the truth in what I was saying.

"At this point, I don't know what to think, I'm just too hurt right now."

"Then do me a favor", I said, as I took her hand, "Just remember what I said."

She turned her head, and abruptly pulled her hand away. It agonized me to see the sadness in her face and to think I was the cause of it.

"I understand if you don't want to talk to me right now, or ever again for that matter, but I think we should talk. Maybe after some time has passed."

There was only silence on her part. I looked at her and then said,

"I guess we should go out, before they start talking about us."

"You go. I'll be out in a minute."

I knew she didn't want to be seen with swollen eyes. She would take a few minutes and then slip imperceptibly into the crowd when they had forgotten about her.

"I'll keep in touch."

That was a lie. If there was to be no future between us, I wanted to forget her. I knew that I could become an obsessive fool, trying to get her back, and she would never accept me back. I would agonize less if I just made a clean break...maybe.

10

I had just finished cleaning up the last of the clutter from the "get-together", when the phone rang. I was so emotionally drained I let the answering machine take it, as I tied yet another plastic garbage bag. "Jefe?" there was a small pause, then again, "Jefe?" another pause and then in Spanish, "I just wanted to talk to you about the little gift package I found in the river." I jumped to the phone and picked it up.

"Hello!"

"Oh, so you *are* there. I was afraid I had missed you."

I had been praying for this call. Andres had been instructed that if he were ever contacted again, he should tell the caller to call me, and to give a safe number where he could reach me. He had been instructed to address me as *Jefe* (Chief) so I could recognize that the call was legitimate. The number that I had given for the call was to a clean, untraceable phone with a built in jamming device which was the one I had picked up on. The call meant my cover would not be blown after this assignment, or at least, I hoped so.

The call had come out of the blue. Apparently he had contacted Andres this morning and had immediately used the information to contact me. We had worked out what we would do in this eventuality.

"You know who I am? You have no doubt?"

"Yes, I know who you are, I have no doubts. There are very few people who know about our little problem in the river or to be more exact, just one."

I could hear him chuckle on the other end of the line.

"By the way, what's your name?"

Another chuckle.

"Let's just stay with *el Cachorro*."

I knew he wasn't going to tell me his name but I needed to verify his pseudonym and he knew this.

"*Jefe*, I don't want to waste time so I am going straight to the point, here's the deal, I want 5 million dollars for the papers and your troubles will be over."

This was a drop in the bucket for the sum we had been anticipating, but I still needed to negotiate, to make him see we were serious.

"We were thinking a lot smaller, perhaps along the line of one million dollars."

Again the chuckle.

"*Jefe*, we both know that this information is worth much more. I could ask in the billions, and you would have to pay it, but I am not a greedy person. I am not being benevolent either, for I know it is easier for you to put together the smaller sum of money, and the search for me would not be as intense afterwards. Besides, I have always been a poor man *Jefe*, and that amount will suit me just fine. "

"You'll make me cry in a minute. Look, I don't want to prolong this either you have us over a barrel. We have to agree to your terms. Now, how do we do this?"

"Well, we are very anxious, aren't we?"

He was toying with me. I said nothing. He probably sensed my irritation and replied.

"Very well, here are the details. I know you are recording this so I will not repeat myself. This coming Thursday I will be waiting at *San Cristobal* fort. This is where the transaction will take place. You are to come personally, you are to come alone. Bring one million in used one hundred dollar bills, another two million in very high quality diamonds and the rest you will put into an account via a wire transfer to the *Bank of the Carribean* in the Cayman Islands; the account is set up in the name of *Cachorro Trading* and the account number is AZ100368–C. I will be monitoring the account to verify that the transaction has taken place. Once I have confirmed the transaction, which should be done early Thursday, you will wait until precisely two in the afternoon and then you are to enter the *San Cristobal* fort through the main gate and proceed to *La Garita del Diablo*. I know that *La Garita* is closed to the public, but I trust that you will find the means of getting through to it. You will wait there and you will be contacted. Another thing, you must wear a blue beret so that you can be identified. It's that simple and of course, if I see anything suspicious the whole transaction will be aborted and I move on to another buyer."

"That's a varied little goodies package you want there and bulky."

"You'll manage."

"How do I get the papers?"

"Once I verify payment, I will disclose their location."

"How can I trust you?"

"You can't. I cannot trust you, but we operate in a distrustful society and we still manage to get things done. Don't we?"

He was right. There were no guarantees in this business.

"I'll see you Thursday."

"And *Jefe?*"

"Yes."

"No bullshit. As I said, if I see anything out of the ordinary the information will be sold to another party."

"I understand."

"I'm glad we have come to an understanding."

With that, there was a click and the conversation was over.

I had three days to make preparations.

11

'It's not that crowded', was the thought that prevailed in my mind that Thursday as I ambled in through the entryway of the *San Cristobal* fort. The fact that the fort was nearly deserted was good, in case there were any problems, there would be fewer innocent people in harm's way. It was one of the rare occasions where there were no cruise ships in the harbor, and also it was a work day on the island which accounted for the sparse number of visitors. So far, so good. I felt really stupid wearing the beret I had bought at one of the many tourist trap shops on *San Justo Street*, but it was a small sacrifice I had to make if it led to the papers being recovered. The entranceway to the fort was alongside an old narrow cobblestone paved street, and we didn't know how sophisticated the surveillance on us was going to be, and we couldn't take the risk of losing the papers because of the presence of a large group of our people who would have stuck out like a sore thumb amongst the sparse number of visitors today. Due to this, the only inside people I had were a pair of local agents posing as a "tourist" couple. To avoid spooking the seller they would be my only immediate backup. We did have a helicopter on call, and the Coast Guard had guaranteed the *Reef Shark,* a patrol boat, to be on a loose watch off the San Juan Bay. There were also several cars in radio contact waiting to take up pursuit in the Municipal parking garage near the main plaza. Frankly, I didn't see how our seller was planning to escape. The passage way to the lower level sentry box was closed to the public because of safety concerns due to its proximity to the sea, and the rocks that surrounded it which became treacherously slippery when wet. I could have arranged for it to be opened, but we wanted the operation to be as secretive as possible, so the agents posing as tourists, as per plan, engaged the three fort security guards at the entrance in some questions and I slipped around them and made my way to the iron gate at the corridor leading to the ancient seaside sentry post. I easily picked the sturdy looking, but simple lock and opened the gate and eased myself into the shadows beyond.

At the far end I could see la *Garita del Diablo* (the Devil's sentry box). It had been so named because in the 1700's, as legend had it, a sentry had been on the watch during the night, in this the most remote outpost of the fort, outside of, and far below its main wall right at ocean side. The night sentries would look over the parapet walls at the lonely sentry box far below and pity the soldier who had duty on that unwanted post. On the particular night in question, the pitied sentry was Sanchez, whom because of his pale white skin, had earned the unenviable nickname of "Orange Blossom". During the night, calls were made to him, as was the custom, but no replies came from the sentry box near the sea. The next morning, after a worried commander had dispatched a soldier to the sentry box, it was found, to his astonishment, completely empty. The guard had seemingly disappeared into thin air. His uniform and musket were found on the ground of the sentry box, and some of the more superstitious soldiers circulated stories that he had been taken by the Devil. Later on, the truth was learned. It seems the Spanish soldier had fallen in love with the daughter of one of the indigenous women on the island. She was a beautiful *mestiza,* half Spanish half native Caribe Indian named Dina. He would strum his guitar and sing love songs to her during the warm tropical nights from the sentry box overlooking the sea. The other sentries grew accustomed to hearing the amorous songs coming from the post on the lower level. One night the *mestiza* girl heard a song different from the ones she had heard before. As she listened to the words, she realized that it was an invitation for her to run away with him on the morrow. The next night, she snuck down the shoreline towards her lover. There, amongst kisses and tender words they made vows to each other, and he changed into the clothes that she had bought him so that he would be disguised, and they ran down the shore, unseen under the cover of night, away from the fort, and disappeared into the blackness. Years later, it was rumored that the lovers had been spotted in a small house deep in the central mountains of the island, where, as these stories usually end, they lived happily ever after.

I approached the ancient guard house. I looked out from the corridor leading from the main building. It was a blinding sunny day. On either side ending at the entrance to the box there were two ancient parapet walls converging into a V shape with the entrance to the small round sentry box at its apex. I peered nervously down the path and could only make out blackness and shadows at the entrance of the sentry box. I wondered if our friend was late for the rendezvous. I started across with a hand on my gun. My heart was pounding, my mouth was dry, and my nerves were on overdrive. If he wanted to shoot me, I was a sitting duck target in this small triangle of earth and grass. Everything was silent; the only sound was of the strong ocean breezes as they gusted. I edged carefully towards the dark opening, my shoulder against the wall to offer a smaller target, just in case. The intensely bright sunshine was blinding me to what was inside, and it was only when I got within three feet of the narrow square entryway, was I able to see somewhat. I could barely make out the concrete interior mottled with age. Taking my gun out I entered cautiously and saw nothing. There was no one. I was perplexed. Perhaps he was late. Suddenly I heard a high pitched prolonged scream from above me. I rushed out and looked up at the imposing fort wall above me. There was another sentry box at the upper level wall, more than a 150 feet up above me, part of the main fort wall. A woman tourist with a pale face was pointing downward, and soon she was joined by two or three more shocked faces. I found myself looking at the soles of a pair of shoes. It seemed that Mr. Irizarry hadn't been late after all. He was hanging by his neck from the sentry box on the wall and twisting ever so slightly in the warm Caribbean breeze.

12

I was on a secure line with Mr. Gardner. I had dreaded making this call, but this was a development he had to know about.

"He was killed without anyone seeing anything?" he asked in astonishment.

"As I mentioned before, Mr. Gardner, we had two agents acting as a tourist couple, but we couldn't risk any more people because it was midweek and the place was relatively empty. We would have risked frightening the suspect away, and as I mentioned, we had a loose Coast Guard surveillance which would have reported anything unusual along the shoreline. I don't know how, but in some fashion the killer managed to slip through all of this and escape undetected."

"I'm traveling there tomorrow. This is a matter of top priority, and we have to have a face to face. I want you to work closely with your San Juan officer, whom I understand is Gina Villegas, right?"

Reluctantly, I replied, "Yes sir."

"Well please call her up and set up a meeting at the usual place for 9:00 am."

"Yes sir."

"Until tomorrow then."

And with that he hung up the phone. This certainly was ironic I mused. I had Gina relocated as far away from me as possible and here I was assigned to work with her tomorrow. The irony of life. Was I sad? Not really. In fact, I was glad to be forced to work with her, I could say even ecstatic. If that wasn't love, I don't know what was.

The next morning we were there at the table, Mr. Gardner, Gina, and I, along with crumpled bagel sandwich wrappers. We sat around sipping our coffees, and trying to come up with a plan to defeat evil intentions in the Caribbean. I was severely limited in this endeavor however, because my mind was constantly diverted to Gina. I was sneaking glances at her and trying to read into her little world.

"So in conclusion, what you're saying is that we're forced to wait again. Have I understood that correctly?" asked Mr. Gardner.

"Yes sir," I replied, "We found out that Mr. Irizarry had ties to Cuba and was a low level spy for the Cuban government. Apparently he acquired that packet by happening upon the crash site, since his cover was being a *publico* driver, and apparently he just found the packet by coincidence and got greedy and tried to profit from it, but he was outed, and we don't know by whom. Until whoever has the information now communicates with us, we have nothing to go on, unless of course, we get a lucky break from an informant, which, if we're dealing with professionals, which I would say we are, is extremely unlikely."

"I have everybody in the metro area on extreme alert." Gina chimed in.

"Well," Mr. Gardner said as he stuffed folders into his attaché case, "this will be our top priority until it is resolved, and it *will* be resolved one way or another. I don't have to mention that you two will be my eyes and ears on this. I'll keep in touch, and I want to be informed immediately of any new development."

With that he smiled at me, shook my hand and Gina's, and left. I watched idly through the window as he approached the Hughes 500P helicopter waiting outside, boarded it, and took off.

I glanced at Gina. She also was looking at the helicopter as it took off. The soft light of the open window, her wide eyes, and her partially open soft full lips, were just too irresistible to me, and against my will, I glided over to her and put one hand around her waist and with the other took her hand into mine. She trembled a bit and I felt her resist. After a few seconds she turned slightly and asked softly, "What are you doing?"

"I just couldn't help myself, you looked too damn gorgeous."

"Let me set one thing straight," she said, as she turned and looked straight into my eyes, "We're assigned to work together, and I will, because that's my job, and you will have my full coopera-tion in that aspect, but as to any personal relationship between us, I'm sorry, but you're going to have to consider that a closed book."

She carefully extricated herself from my hold as she said this and stood facing me.

I felt as if a glass of cold water had been dashed in my face.

"OK, I understand, I just missed you, that's all. But I promise, from now on, strictly professional."

She seemed a little shaken, and we both picked up our papers in silence. I knew it was going to be a very uncomfortable situation for both of us.

"Will you accept lunch Gina?, its company money, not mine, just an opportunity to discuss what we do next, strictly professional."

She looked at me as I to fathom if I was serious. I was, and apparently she saw that and agreed.

"We have a lot to go over, and we have to plan some kind of initiative, so I guess we can start over lunch, as long as the company is picking up the tab."

"It is", I answered with a wry smile.

And with that we both walked out together.

During our lunch, we came to the conclusion that it was impossible to pursue ghosts. Until we had something else to go on, we had to be necessarily reactive, so our best plan was to be prepared for several likely eventualities. Our best hope, was that we made contact with whoever had the papers, or even better yet, a leak of information leading to the party that had the information would be provided through our net of informants to one of our agents. We also had to step from a passive role and step into a more active one. We had to try to develop leads as to who had taken the papers and how they had learned that Irizarry had them in the first place. I had contacts and people I used in Utuado where Irizarry had worked and lived, so I would try to flush out some information from that angle, and Gina had, of course, the San Juan metro area contacts, and she would try to find out any information from this source. Having defined our agendas for the immediate future, we ended lunch and I watched her walk down *El Paseo de la Princesa*, a waterfront walkway bordering the San Juan Bay. She looked like a goddess as she walked down the promenade, in the hot tropical sun and I watched her as she made her way to the end and disappeared around the corner. Snapping out of it, I went towards the municipal garage to get my car and start the long drive back to Guanica bay.

13

Unbelievably, not 24 hours had passed before I had two very good leads regarding information on who had killed Mr. Irizarry and made off with the papers. The first lead came from one of Gina's contacts. He said that he had been drinking in one of the local watering holes and had overheard a conversation between two heavyset gentlemen in a booth behind him. Normally, this wouldn't have attracted his attention, but they were speaking a foreign language and trying to talk in a hushed tone, which due to the high level of voices from the crowd in the bar was impossible, so that they ended up having to shout out repeated replies. The informant had casually looked behind him and saw two heavyset gentlemen. Having spent a good deal of time at the Puerto Nuevo docks, and having seen sailors of all nationalities, he ventured a guess that these were Russian. After a while, he decided to get up and use the bathroom, and as he turned in a sudden movement he startled one of the men who hastily turned a photo on the table face down, but not before the contact had seen it. He acted as though he were indifferent to the whole incident and used the bathroom and came back and stayed until he saw the two men leave. He waited another hour, and as an extra precaution made friends with a group of five men who worked together and were out for an evening of bar hopping, and left with them, being sure to be in the center of the group using them as camouflage. He reached his apartment safely and quickly proceeded to call the office and tell them about the incident and the picture he had seen; a picture of Gina.

The second lead was more substantial and more to the point. A short while after I had been made aware of the report from the contact, I got a call on my office hot line. I was surprised. It probably was Gardner wanting to be updated on what was going on. I picked up the phone and heard a male's voice with a heavy accent, which I immediately identified as Russian, ask,

"Mr. Hines?"

"Yes, who is this?"

"I am glad we could reach you on the first try. Just call me Mr. X. I am calling you because we have something that can be of great interest to you."

"Who is this, what do you want?"

"Very simply put we want to negotiate. We picked up some papers from someone who happened to be hanging around the San Cristobal fort, and we believe that they are of interest to you."

I was instantly alert. There was a pause as I digested the situation.

"By the way, Mr. Hines, do no attempt to trace this call because if you do, it will lead you to an empty public phone booth. You would be very disappointed and you will have wasted a lot of valuable time. Also you would be putting the life of a very dear friend in grave danger. In fact, let me have her speak with you."

"Matt! I'm O.K., don't-"

Gina's voice was abruptly cut off.

"What is this?" I yelled into the phone, "What do you want?"

"Just a little bit of insurance Mr. Hines, just insurance. As I said before, all we want is to negotiate some terms that will be agreeable to both of us."

"What exactly do you want?" I asked icily.

"Mr. Hines, we wish to do no damage, all we want is a satisfactory monetary arrangement in exchange for the papers and the girl. That's it, simple and sweet. If you act appropriately, then everything can be expedited and all that will remain for you, Mr. Hines, is a faint unpleasant memory."

"What are your terms?"

"The same terms that you were willing to satisfy for Mr. Irizarry, - only quadrupled."

"Are you out of your mind?"

"Come, come, Mr. Hines, you are no longer dealing with an amateur anymore. You well know that this information is worth a lot more than the modest sum I am asking. Besides, your government cannot afford to lose the papers at any cost."

I reflected on that for a moment. He knew I was between a rock and a hard place. His assessment was correct, I *had* to have those papers, and he knew it.

"Who do you work for?"

"You know better than to ask that, Mr. Hines. I may be working on my own, or I may be working on someone's behalf, but that will be my little secret."

"What happens if I pay? What assurance do I have that the information will not be used anyway?"

"We happened to learn the contents of your conversation with Mr. Irizarry, and I am going to tell you the same thing he told you. You just have to trust us. Besides, if the information was leaked, I would be cutting my own throat, as I operate in an area where trust, secrets, and discretion are of paramount importance."

"Let's cut the bull, I would have to OK everything with my superiors, but as you know, we probably will pay because we need the papers, so what now?"

"You make another little trip, with a bigger bag and the money, all of it, will be sent via wire transfer to a different account. When we get the stones and money, you will get the girl and the papers. We have chosen different location for the transfer. It will be done at the Camuy Caverns. You will receive detailed instructions shortly."

"Very well, I'll take a look at them, and Mr. X?"

"Yes?"

"If any harm comes to her, I will hunt you down personally and I will find you."

With that, I hung up.

I sat thinking about what had just happened, when I heard what sounded like a chopper outside. I ran out and looked up. About 300 feet above me was a flying helicopter model. Suddenly, as I watched it, a parachute with a gleaming gray metal canister deployed from it and floated toward me. The model took off towards the north at a fast speed and after a few seconds disappeared from sight and from hearing range. The remote controlled helicopter model had probably been retrieved and its handlers were most likely doing their best to vacate the area as quickly as possible. I went to where the canister had fallen, and unscrewing the cylinder, verified that the instructions for the caverns exchange had indeed been delivered. It would take place on the following day.

All I knew now was that both my phone lines and location had been seriously compromised. I thought of a way where I could gain back some ground. I placed a call on a satellite phone, hoping this wasn't compromised, although it would be very hard because this line was password protected for extra security. I called my friend at the National Reconnaissance Office, a sort of catch-all agency that supplied satellite intel for a lot of Uncle Sam's organizations including the CIA, NSA, Department of Defense, and others while somehow managing to stay, for the most part, out of the public eye. I was lucky to reach Micky on my first try. Usually I had to page him or leave voice messages until he contacted me. I explained what I needed and he told me he would get back to me as soon as possible as to whether he could be of assistance or not on my request.

About three quarters of an hour later he called me back and gave me some good news. It seemed that my area had been covered at the time of the message incident by not only one, but two satellites, one being a GOES weather satellite, that in this case was doubling as a spy satellite. He was sending me images of the flight of the model chopper and more importantly the image of where the flight originated and ended. Apparently the model had flown across Guanica bay to a red Toyota Tacoma pickup that had been waiting on a shoreline road, where it landed and was retrieved. The truck had then sped way. It was tracked heading towards Ponce, but then the satellite was lost to the tracking system. The pickup was later identified as a '97 model. One enlarged frame of the video feed was of a rear view image of the truck and had shown two distinctive decals, one of India beer, (a previous local brew, now defunct), and one from the University of Puerto Rico. Not exactly a spy vehicle. My suspicions were confirmed hours later when the truck was matched against a report of a recovered stolen vehicle from the nearby Mayaguez police department. It was our truck. Against the vociferous protests of the owner who had come to pick it up, the pickup was processed, but as expected, yielded no prints or any usable forensic evidence.

14

The Camuy Caverns are located in the central northern part of the island, near its namesake, the town of Camuy. The part of the caverns open to the public, is situated along one of the entryway roads to the island's central mountain region amid splendid tropical vegetation and karst rock formations. The modern day, government-owned park encompasses 268 acres of mountains, ravines, and otherwise rugged terrain. Because of this, there was no way we could set up a complete and thorough surveillance of the area, which was why the usual warning of not coming accompanied was not given in the phone call I had received. I was dealing with a professional. This was someone who definitely knew what he was doing.

As per instructions, I arrived at 1:00 in the afternoon. I got in line with the local and American tourists. The wire transfer had already been confirmed and in a knapsack on my back was a packet containing four million dollars worth of rough cut, high quality diamonds. I hoped the knapsack wouldn't attract attention, but I need not have worried. Most of the tourists were carrying, camera bags, coolers, or a bag of one type or other. I was waiting to be picked up by a tram that was to take us from the elevated ticketing point to the entrance of the caverns, which was at a lower level.

The tram station was a wooden structure, built in a rustic lumber style, and consisted of the waiting area, a gift shop, cafeteria, and ticketing booths. It was surrounded by fountains and exotic plant gardens. Nestled in between the mountains, it looked like a little tropical oasis. Per instructions I was just to take the tour like any other tourist, and I would be contacted at any time. I didn't know if I was going to be contacted at ticketing, on the tram, in the caverns, or for that matter, if I would be contacted at all. I was ill at ease, and suspected anyone within my general area of being the person I was to meet and I would casually scrutinize them. I could go crazy acting this way.

After a wait of several minutes, the tram finally arrived, and I boarded it to begin the 300 foot or so descent to the main entrance of the caverns. The tram followed a narrow inclined paved road that snaked down the mountain side, with sharp drops on either side where one could look down through the lush vegetation, and see hundreds of feet below. A small loudspeaker mounted on the lead car provided the usual tram warnings and a few details of our surroundings. I delighted in the ferns, banana plants, and other dense tropical vegetation on either side, which made this look like a real life Disney ride. At one point the tram path bent back at an almost 180 degree turn, while at a steep descending angle almost turning onto itself. Since there had just been a light rainfall, wetting the pavement and making it slick, I started to worry about the driving experience, (or lack of it), of the tram driver who seemed younger than 18. To my relief, we finally reached the bottom and got out. I looked around, no contact yet. I followed the crowd, which in turn, followed the tour guide for our group, who started spouting cavern information, history, descriptions, and the rest of his usual tourist spiel.

It was silly, under the circumstances, but I was momentarily absorbed in observing a huge spider web built right near the entrance. I approached it to get a close up look. It was the largest web I had ever seen. I looked around and saw that the group was already entering, and I ran to catch up to them. We were led into the first of the cavern chambers. It was huge, and very dark, the only light coming from spotlights that highlighted some of the caverns more unusual formations. The guide mentioned it was the Clara cave, and that it had a 170 foot ceiling. It certainly looked very high. It was very impressive. Everyone talked in whispers or hushed tones. Why did they do this? There was no logical explanation for it. Maybe they were awed by nature and instinctively were humbled by it. It took about 25 minutes to transverse this area. I was nervously looking in all directions for a contact, but possibly because of the dim light, did not see anything, and was not approached by anyone. I knew that I definitely had to be under observation, but if I was, they were pretty good, because I couldn't make out anybody with an unusual interest in me.

After the first part of the cavern, we exited into an open round area, between the first and second main areas of the portion of the cavern system open to tourists. At first the stark contrast between the darkness we had just exited and the bright tropical sun of the outside blinded me, but my eyes adjusted, and I was able to look around. It was an awe inspiring sight. I was in a 400 feet deep sinkhole. I looked up at the sheer rock face all around covered in places by vines, ferns, palms, and other plants typical of this region. The very top edge was surrounded by stands of trees, as if they were centurions standing guard so that no one could escape. Even the light had an unnatural, unreal, quality to it. If there were any claustrophobics in our group they sure would feel queasy in spite of the large area we were in.

The guide for our group led us to a part of the rock wall on one side, which had water cascading down. He explained that it was spring water filtered by its journey through the rock, and therefore purified by nature. He invited everyone to sample the water, and several tourists did. I stood to one side observing them. Which one, if any, was my contact? No one stood out, or looked out of place. Was someone else going to come along? What were they waiting for? I had already been here close to forty minutes. We were about to enter the second section of the caverns on the far side. I entered the new section, the darkness broken only by the yellowish spotlights that gave everything a surreal look. Again following the guide, I trekked to an area surrounded by a guardrail. I looked down and all I could see was a huge dark void. It was the Tres Pueblos sinkhole, so called because it was a natural 400 foot deep sinkhole whose 650 foot diameter encompassed three different municipalities of Puerto Rico, Camuy, Lares, and Hatillo. One could hear the Camuy River rushing far below.

As I was involuntarily engrossed in this sight, I felt someone press close to me, and I heard a male voice say into my ear,

"Follow me Mr. Hines. I'm your contact. I remind you, if you try anything funny, your friend, Ms. Villegas will suffer the consequences."

THE PRESIDENT'S PAPERS

I meekly followed him as he melded into the shadows. At a point that was extremely dark, I saw him seem to disappear. I realized there was an extremely narrow fissure in the rock face. I squeezed through, intent on following. I could hear him scraping through ahead of me. It was pitch black. I pressed against the walls. They were cold and slimy. Probably due to moss growth, or at least that's what I hoped. There was a strong musky stale odor in the air. We must have gone about 100 yards when I noticed that there was a faint light further down the passage. I kept following my contact until I saw him cross the light source and appeared to vanish once again. It wasn't until I reached the same spot that I realized that the opening made a right hand turn, and as I followed, I entered into a large cavern. My eyes automatically sought the light source. On one of the faces of this cave, about 100 yards above me, I saw that there was an opening to the outside. The light was natural sunlight. I could see roots of trees, and vegetation that ascended from the floor of the opening. But what really got my heart pumping, was a ledge in front of the cave opening, and on the ledge was Gina, tied to a wooden post, with a gag covering her mouth. She was flanked by two goons, and in front was the man I had apparently come to talk to. When Gina saw me she reacted by twisting and struggling against her ties. The man just looked at her and smiled. All of a sudden, I was grabbed by the elbows, by two more goons, and searched for weapons. I didn't put up any resistance, and they found my obligatory gun. I had bought my locally procured Colt 45. After satisfying themselves that this was the only firearm I had, they retreated and left me in the center of the cavern. I looked up at my host. He seemed to be, as I had surmised

Russian, with eyes that squinted when he smiled, which he seemed to do quite frequently. He had salt and pepper hair, and mustache, which contrasted sharply with his bushy jet black eyebrows. I calculated he was about '6 "1 and in his late 40's.

"Well, Mr. Hines, I hope the trip here was not too difficult for you, it's hard to find good hidden caves anymore."

As he said this, his eyes crinkled with mirth at his own joke. Then he became serious.

"I trust you have what I asked for?"

"Yes I do. But I've left the items at a hidden location nearby, as a guarantee. So what I suggest is that you come down here with Ms. Villegas and then you follow me to the location, I'll point it out, you verify the contents, give me the memo, and then Gina and I'll go in one direction, and you'll go the opposite direction, a very simple transaction."

I could see him analyzing the proposition and knew he didn't like losing control of the situation, but after some thought he acceded.

"Very well, wait there, I will come down."

A few minutes later, I was reunited in the middle of the cavern with Gina, and surrounded by the Russian, and his men.

"Now we make a little trip to pick up, shall we say, my reward?"

"Let's go."

I got as close to Gina as I could, and turned towards the cavern entrance. We squeezed out to the main cavern. I grabbed Gina's elbow seemingly to steady her.

With that I pressed the stone on the black onyx ring I was wearing, which contained a signal transmitter. A special park agent had been instructed on what to do. He immediately cut the lights to all the Caverns. Immediately there were cries from all the tourists and locals when they found themselves immersed in total darkness. Even the emergency lights were taken out of action. I had memorized a spot about five steps away behind a huge stalactite, and grabbed Gina and bolted for it. I lay low and succeeded in temporarily losing my forced bodyguards. I knew I only had one minute of darkness. The Cavern administration had been firm on this point; they couldn't risk the safety of the visitors. I could hear one of the guides, using his battery powered megaphone, exhorting everyone to stay calm, and reassuring everyone that the lights would come on again shortly.

Gina had realized that this was an escape intent, and had remained silent, so as not to give our position away. I reached for my innocent looking "sunglasses" which had been in my shirt pocket, hiding in plain view. I put them on and saw the marks. The heel of one of my shoes had been prepared by our tech division to contain a plastic bladder containing a clear infrared liquid a drop of which was released with every step I had taken. The polarized "sunglasses", permitted me to see the trail of markings, and I rushed with Gina, to the narrow entrance, and was able to squeeze through and reach the exit to the main cavern before the lights came back on.

After the sixty seconds had elapsed, the lights were turned back on. The would be kidnappers must have been bewildered to find me gone as if by magic. They would soon realize that I probably was out by now and soon would be in pursuit. I had to hurry. There were five other people from my group mixed in with the tourists and at least one of them should have spotted me. I didn't have time to wait around and see if they had. I pulled Gina after me and told her she had to run for her life. I looked back and the Russian group spilled out all of a sudden from the crevice like angry hornets from a nest. They seemed to have guns drawn. They were not going to play nice. Because of the dim lighting they couldn't see us immediately, but after a few seconds something gave us away. It could have been my gait, Gina's outline, or any of a number of things. The fact was that all of a sudden a call went out from one of the group, and they started running en masse in our direction. With the dimness it appeared they would lose sight of us, but then, just as suddenly, they would see us again. We neared the open area between the two caves.

I told Gina to run as fast as she could because we were exposed in the outside daylight. We made a beeline for the first cavern. As we entered the first cave I looked back as our pursuers erupted from the second cave into the sunlight. They took a few seconds to adjust to the sunlight and then quickly spotted us and started after us once again. Suddenly someone came flying at them from the side and knocked two of the five men over and he was joined quickly by another helper. My team had arrived. They couldn't use firearms in a public place so it boiled down to an old fashioned fist fight. People started screaming and security personnel started running towards the commotion from inside the cavern I was entering. This was great for us. We started crossing the cavern to get to the main entrance. We were both breathing hard and blood was pulsing hard in our temples, but we were almost there. I kept looking back and saw no one in pursuit. We were suddenly at the exit and I looked back and saw, as if by magic, two of our pursuers appear from the crowd behind us and about 50 yards away.

I exited into the daylight holding Gina by the hand. I was panicking now. I looked around desperately and saw that a tram had just emptied and the driver had gotten off to assist the last passenger, an elderly gentleman, with an electric wheelchair. We rushed towards it and as soon as the driver wheeled the older passenger some distance away, I jumped into the driver's seat at the same time shouting at Gina to get in. She jumped into the first row of seats and I floored the accelerator, and we were off with a jolt. The operator realized what was happening to late and couldn't leap back on, but unseen by either of us, one of the last pursuers had managed to grab on to the last car and get a foothold on the bumper. I concentrated on taking the uphill closed curve as fast as I could without overturning or landing in any of the ravines.

Gina was crouched over me from the seat behind. She turned to see if anyone was running after us just in time to see our new friend swing over a seat row in the last car.

"Matthew!"

Her scream almost made me lose control. I glanced at where she pointed and saw him advancing.

"Do you think you can manage to drive this?", I shouted.

She nodded in the affirmative.

"Then here, let's switch."

We awkwardly traded positions as I tried to keep steering and at the same time vacate my seat. Gina meantime slid in and took over. I looked back again. There were four cars and already our friend was jumping into the third one. We were at the top of the mountain. Our pursuer had managed to temporarily brace himself and I saw the gun in his hand and ducked. Splinters flew from where my body had been seconds before. I cautiously looked from one side and saw him instantly aim and fire again. Once again, that corner of the seat dissolved into fragments. Gina had seen this and suddenly veered sharply to one side, throwing the Russian off balance and making him loose his footing and fall. I had anticipated her move and was able to hook my arm around a handrail and was thus able to recover faster. I quickly looked down at the connection between the cars and bent over and slid the bolt holder out and the engine car was freed. The Russian realized too late what I had done and tried to jump, but the sudden shift of direction made him fall backward as the cars raced to the bottom again. They reached the closed curve portion, and I watched in fascination as the cars continued in a straight line, over the precipice and tumbled head over heels down the rocky slope. I saw a body flung out and then the car behind slam into it as it continued sliding downward, so much for our friend.

We continued onward and without the weight of the extra cars the engine speed picked up considerably. We drove up to the parking lot and got as close to my car as possible. Gina stopped the tram with a jerk and we both jumped out and raced to my vehicle. Apparently no one from the bottom had managed to communicate what had happened to the top because there wasn't anybody running after us. I turned the car on and sped out of there as fast as I could. We reached state road 454 and I turned east and headed towards our San Juan office. I phoned the other men and verified that they had apprehended the other players in this drama except for the apparent leader of the group who somehow managed to wrest himself from the grip of Lenny, (one of my agents), and had disappeared. The prisoners would be brought to San Juan and interrogated. There was nothing to go back for except risking to be held by the local authorities, so we decided to press on to San Juan.

I glanced over at Gina and she was looking at me at the same time. This pleased me immensely. She gave me a small smile and whispered, "Thank you." It seemed a little forced, but it was a thank you just the same.

"You're welcome. Any time at all. Are you all right?" I asked.

"I've been better, but yes, I'm OK."

We were both shaking from the close call.

"What happened? How did they get you?"

"Well, I went on my routine lunch break. I was walking to 'El Patio De Sam' when a van came to the curb, and suddenly I felt someone grab me from behind as he covered my mouth and at the same time the sliding door was opened and I was shoved in and handcuffed before I knew what was happening. They blindfolded me, my heart felt like it was going to jump out of my chest, and I started sweating. We drove and, by the sounds, I could tell that we were leaving the city. I was taken to some rural area, I could tell by the lack of traffic sounds and by the sounds of cows. It was about a two hour drive. When we stopped I was dragged by the men up some steps and into a room. I was let loose only because they knew I couldn't escape. There was a steel door with no latch, doorknob, or anything to try to jimmy on the inside. It was so well fitted to the frame that I couldn't have fit a sheet of paper through it. The only opening was a small barred window about 12 feet above the floor, that I had no possibility of reaching and even if I did, I would have still had to deal with the bars which looked pretty solid. The only furniture in the room was a canvas cot, and a metal mirror, fastened to the wall. Looking out I confirmed that I seemed to be in the country. I saw tree branches and could hear birds and the wind would gust from time to time and could hear it move through the tree limbs. There were no car or people sounds, I was completely isolated. I could have screamed but that probably would have resulted in an unwelcome visit, and besides, seeing what I had seen through the window, it was highly unlikely there was anyone around to hear me. They had probably picked this location precisely because of this.

After about an hour, they opened a hatch in the door and slid in a metal tray with some *arroz con gandules* and a coke, I must say, the food wasn't that bad, but I was so scared I couldn't really enjoy it. Soon darkness came, and I thought I'd be much too afraid to sleep, but with all the silence, and the breeze coming in from the window, I was asleep within the hour. When I awoke, it was morning, and I was ravenous. After about an hour they bought me a huge breakfast, everything I could have whatever I wanted; bacon, eggs, juice, coffee, and buttered toasted Cuban bread. I started eating, and all of a sudden I started feeling sleeping and realized I must have been sedated with something in the food. Next thing I know, I'm in the back of a car or truck again, blindfolded and traveling. I still was sedated and drifted back into sleep, and when I woke up, I'm standing at the cave ledge and I saw you there below me, and you know the rest."

"Well I'm glad I was able to drop by." I said, glancing sideways at her.

"So am I.", she replied as she looked at me.

The tension between us built up. I didn't want to say anything because I was afraid I'd offend her, and I didn't want to start down that path again.

"Well, we'll just amble on to the office and write a report."

"Matt."

I looked at her and saw that she was looking very serious. I sensed that she was struggling to articulate some thought in the proper way.

"I'm really thankful that you cared for me. I really appreciate it. It doesn't erase what happened, it just doesn't work like that," she said pensively, "but at least what you did, shows that you care for me, and it alleviates some of the pain. I just wanted to tell you that because it seems silly that we both should sit here and pretend nothing's happened."

I pulled to the side and stopped the car and turned to face her.

Looking into her eyes I said "Gina, you know how I feel about you, and believe me, what I did, wasn't a stunt to force you to feel obligated to me. I just wanted to get you out of danger because I do want to protect you regardless of what happens after."

"I know, and as I said I appreciate it. I still feel hurt, but maybe with time things can change."

"I'm glad you said that and we can be frank because sometimes these things are left unsaid and then neither one of us knows how we stand in regard to each other."

She gave me a small smile. I looked longingly into her eyes and then turned and started the car. Something had changed and I felt it was for the better, and I felt happy.

15

As I opened the door to the office, the inevitable happened. The secure line rang. I knew that as soon as Mr. Gardner found out about the incident, I'd be hearing from him. He must have been calling at frequent intervals due to the fact, that because of the security measures, the secure line did not have any kind of voice mail device. He sure was anxious to learn the details. I rushed in and picked up.

"Hello, Hines here."

"Hello Matt, its Mr. Gardner"

"Hello Mr. Gardner, I was going to call you, I just arrived from Camuy, and literally was just walking through the door."

"Well this is a top priority case and I heard some details about the botched exchange and just wanted to keep tabs on what went on. How's Gina?"

"She's alive and well, a little shaken, but she suffered no physical injuries. In fact she's right here, would you like to talk to her?"

"Yes, let me have a word with her."

"Hello, Sir."

"Hello Gina," Gardner replied, "I just wanted to see how you were."

PEDRO VARGAS

"Like Matt said, just a few bruises, but nothing major. I guess the fright I was put through was worse than the actual ordeal, but thanks to him and the other boys I survived."

"Well I'm glad you're well, and I'm sorry you had to go through that. We'll review policies and procedures to try to avoid that sort of thing happening again. Now, reluctantly, I'm going to have to bring up some work matters. What happened to the papers? Do you know?"

Gina looked at me, and I nodded affirmatively, and she started a narrative of everything that had happened, ending with,

"So as you see, to the best of my knowledge, the leader of the band of hoodlums, escaped with the papers still in his possession."

"I see, well thank you again for your service, and I hope you're completely recovered in record time."

"Thank you."

"You're more than welcome; can I speak to Matt again?"

"Sure," covering the phone speaker she beckoned, "Matt, you again!"

Handing me the phone again, I said,

"Mr. Gardner."

"I of course, want a full written report, but most of all, I want identification of the people in custody, and leads on what happened to the papers."

"We'll write a full report and submit it to you within the hour, that's why I'm here with Gina, and then I'll see what we can learn from the prisoner interrogation, and I'll get back to you as soon as we're done."

"I appreciate that; until I hear from you then."

And with that there was a click, and Mr. Gardner was off the line.

I looked at Gina and she just smiled, just like old times, and my heart soared. I had to keep my mind on the work at hand.

"I guess we have a report to write."

"Let's get to it."

For the next forty minutes we were busy refreshing each other's memories and redacting the report on my laptop. I could feel her warmth behind me as she would lean over to look at what had been written. I felt like I was in my private little paradise.

Of course, paradisiacal conditions don't last forever, and this was no exception. Just when I was thinking of speaking to Gina and saying something personal, and making a fool of myself once again, one of the office lines rang. I picked up on the second ring.

"Hello, Hines here."

"Matt!" I recognized the voice. It was Stewart, one of my office staff, who in conjunction with some of our people sent from Virginia, had been interrogating the prisoners.

"What's up?"

"We are in the process of interrogating a certain Dima Andreev, and after graciously telling us his name, he mentioned the fact that the group had a safe house from which they were operating locally in the Dos Bocas lake area."

"Do you know exactly where?"

"Come on Matt, it's me baby, you know how I work."

Yes, I did know how he worked. Stewart would have obtained the information. These prisoners should have been treated with diplomatic gloves, but life in the Russian KBG was hard, and knowing this, as soon as they were caught they would be threatened with deportation, or with threats of creating false leaks from information obtained from other sources, pointing the finger at them as the source, which if not causing their death, would at least severely hamper their chances of continuing to serve as agents, effectively terminating their career. But in cases where death had already occurred, such as this one, and information was vitally needed, Stewart would use other means. He would send another of his agents in who would point out the obvious fact that there had been deaths, that there were plenty of civilian witnesses to the fact, and that to these people, one Russian looked like the other, so that if someone else from the group died, it could easily be explained away as someone who had died in the initial encounter. This was clearly communicated to the unfortunate prisoner and usually emphasized by blows to the body and face.

"No one cares if you die." he would be told, and then he would be reminded of what awaited them if they returned. They would be disgraced, and reprimanded for a botched up job, or worse. By this time they usually would be badly shaken up. Being isolated they had no one to confer with. At this point the agent would leave the room and he would let them stew for a while. Then Steward would enter the room and with a paternal smile put a hand on their shoulder, look them in the eye, and say something to the effect

"Look, this doesn't have to be like this." Then he would offer them economic incentives, a new home, a new life. And once in a while it worked. Yes, I knew how Stewart worked, but I preferred not to know, at least officially. If the Soviets found out they could put up a big stink, but we had plenty of things on them that they had attempted, so it was par for the course. They could only stew and wait for an opportunity for revenge.

In this case Stewart's methods had yielded positive results. The Russian that Stewart had targeted, was young, had no immediate family alive in Russia, and had felt snubbed by the KGB. He had been a great candidate to turn, and turn he did. He would be a American taxpayer's burden from now on, but we really needed the information he had in the shortest time possible. To me, the payoff was worth it.

"It seems they established a safe house and had been operating there for the last two weeks or so."

"And where is it?" I asked my pulse racing with excitement.

"Well believe it or not, they didn't use coordinates, but he tells me it was located exactly 1.28 miles from the split on Route 10, at the beginning of the *Dos Bocas* lake."

Dos Bocas literally meant two mouths, and was thus named because the area that carried this name was actually two lakes that fed into one river, and one portion of the lakes, was in itself linked to another lake, *Lago Caonillas,* which formed part of the water system where the plane had originally gone down, causing this whole mess. The area was rugged and mountainous, and sparsely inhabited. No one would have noticed the strangers passing by in a tinted glass SUV, which was the preferred type of vehicle in this area. It wouldn't have seemed out of place.

"We're going to make a little visit then, and I want you in on it and certainly myself, and two others in one car, and another car with four more people. I want full body armor, some big guns, and a full complement of things that go boom."

Stewart chuckled.

"Will do boss. When do we make the hit?"

"Let's say we meet at 6:00 am at the Arecibo Caribbean Cinemas parking lot."

"Those are the ones on interstate No.2, right"

"Those are the ones."

"I'll talk with Gina, so she can run communications at the office, in case we have to call in for extra help."

We had talked to the local DEA and reluctantly, they had offered to be on call with one of their drug intercepting helicopters in case we were outgunned and needed reinforcements.

"See you there at six; I'll round up the rest of the guys."

16

Arecibo was the third largest city in Puerto Rico, and was about 90 minutes east of San Juan. The town was readily accessible from anywhere on the island and the fact that the old Route 10, the road to the Russian base of operations, initiated from it, made me pick it as our coordinating point.

At 5:30am I was already at the parking lot waiting for the other guys. I was parked northward, facing the cinema building so I had a view of the white sand beach at a distance behind it, bordered by coconut palms, and the Atlantic Ocean, which to me, achieved the most beautiful blue at this spot more than any other shore it ever touched. The sun was just coming up, with a spectacular display of orange, yellows, reds, and the contrasting blues. The scene outshone any of the ones found on the myriads of tourist postcards. It was a peaceful, serene start to the day. I sat back in the car and relaxed. A little time after, a red Mitsubishi Eclipse slid into the spot next to me. It was Stewart. He had left Gina overseeing the prisoner interrogation, because he wanted to be in on the action. Knowing him, nothing would have kept him away.

Leaving my car, I shook hands with him.

"Good morning! Good day for bear hunting" I said grinning at him.

"You better believe it. I'm ready to go. Let's get it on!"

"We have to wait for the others; you're too weak to take them on by yourself."

Actually, Stewart worked out religiously and had the best physical shape of anyone I knew.

He feigned outrage at my words.

"Are you saying I can't take those little wimps by myself? Let me at them."

"We'll see, just the same, I'm going to wait for help."

The others filtered in little by little and were all there before six. Two of the eight had come in the Company vehicles, identical beige Land Rovers. I checked inside to verify we were prepared.

"You think we have enough toys?" Stewart asked as he came up behind me.

"You know what they say; you can never have enough toys." I replied with a smile.

There was a virtual arsenal; concussion grenades, assorted handguns, mortars, and other assault weapons. I made sure there were enough Kevlar vests and helmets for everyone and the radio sets to talk with each other to be put on once we reached the proximity of the premises. I calmed everyone down, divided everyone into two groups, and we started rolling.

After thirty minutes the roadside scenery on Route 10, started to become more and more rural. The old Route 10 road had been replaced by a modern four lane expressway, so that the old winding two lane road we were on fell into disuse and it was in bad shape. It meandered through neglected countryside and only the lonely house here and there was witness to our little cavalcade. Even at this early morning hour, the heat was starting to become unbearable. Pretty soon, we were traveling through 6 foot tall clumps of elephant grass that bordered each side of the narrow road. On our right side, from time to time, there would be a break in the grass and we could catch a glimpse of the lake beyond. Basically, the only line of vision we had was directly straight ahead of us, and because of the curves in the road, that was broken every hundred yards or so. I began to worry of what would happen if a car came from the opposite direction. The road was so narrow; I don't think two of us could have been able to squeeze by at the same time. Someone would have to back up to the nearest wide portion to let the other pass. As luck would have it, we didn't encounter any other vehicles.

After a few minutes of driving, our GPS system indicated that the turn-off road to our destination was approaching. We slowed down, and I saw it; a narrow dirt road to the left. We turned in and traveled the dusty strip. Turning around a bend in the road I glimpsed the house about two hundred yards ahead of us. It was a medium size plantation style two-story wooden house. The top floor had a balcony that ran the entire length of the house and had two doors and four windows. The first floor had another length wide balcony and had one main door and two windows on each side. The paint was old and faded, and there were no vehicles in the front yard, only a large *flamboyan* tree around which several hens and a rooster were scattered scratching in the dirt. Everything seemed quiet, maybe too quiet.

I stopped the vehicles. We were semi-hidden by the vegetation. Orders were given, and everyone donned their vests and helmets, and armed themselves according to the pre-established plan. Our approach was simple; my vehicle to the right, the other to the left. Stewart, Anthony, our second man, and I would go in through the front entrance, and Eleazar, our remaining man would guard the left side of the house. Three men from the other vehicle would enter through the back, and the final man would take the right. I repeated the warnings of verifying targets before firing if we came under attack, and the precautions that we needed to take in order to avoid crossfire. We certainly didn't need our own friends killing or wounding us.

As soon as we were set up we reentered the Land Rovers and raced towards the house. I had a heightened alertness, and could feel myself sweating. If we were to encounter resistance, this would be the moment. I glanced to the side. Everyone was tense and concentrated on the task at hand. I expected to feel the explosion of a grenade or the chatter of an automatic rifle at any moment, but we got to the house without incident. My group took up our position veering to the right. The vehicle came to a halt, and we jumped out. Stewart, Manny (who was the second man), and I raced to the front entrance, AK47's at the ready, and with a belt of concussion and smoke grenades. Manny stood at the front door with the "key", a concrete filled 6inch wide steel pipe, with handles welded to the side. With a powerful swing he hit the door right at the juncture of the lock. The flimsy lock sprang open instantly and Manny stood to the side, as he let go the "key" and started to unsling his weapon. Meanwhile, Stewart and I sprang through the doorway, I falling to the floor to the right in a prone position, and Stewart doing the same to the left. This was no social call, so we didn't identify ourselves. If anyone was inside, they would probably be going for their weapons right about now. I could hear the smashing of the rear door going on as the second team entered the rear.

Not encountering resistance, Stewart and I scrambled up immediately and joined by Manny, we slowly advanced through into the interior. Shadows danced against the walls in the bright morning sun. We split. Silently I pointed a door out to each man on either side, and they went through their assigned doors. I kept walking ahead and went through the living room. It was furnished in traditional antique cane-back chairs. Dozens of old photos lined the various tables. I wondered vaguely what had happened to the puertorrican family depicted in the pictures. The pictures suggested several generations had lived here. Everything suddenly became eerily silent. I could even hear morning bird calls outside. The wooden floor squeaked as I tread slowly to the back entrance, I peeked cautiously around the corner and was startled to see one of my own, who had advanced almost to the front. I had unconsciously raised my rifle and had my finger on the trigger. I slowly let the fingers relax on the death grip I had on my weapon. If we weren't careful we would blast each other's head off.

Pretty soon, I heard "Clear, clear", coming from all sides of the house. Everyone checked off their assigned portion of the dwelling. Nobody was home. That really didn't surprise me. After escaping, the lead thug had probably made a beeline to the house, had picked up any incriminating evidence and anyone that stayed on as backup and that had not directly participated in the meeting at the cave. They had probably high-tailed it out a long time before we had arrived. At this moment they were probably headed out to the Dominican Republic, Venezuela, or any of the surrounding countries that were sympathetic to Russia and were they could bribe themselves into.

Manny smiled at me and said,

"It looks like we got invited after the party was over!"

"The bastards are probably flying first class to Moscow, right now." interjected Stewart.

"Yeah,", and after I looked around me, I added, "well let's finish the job"

We then next proceeded to the next phase, a thorough search for any papers, personal items, basically anything left behind in haste that could serve as a lead or could give us an explanation of what had happened.

Anthony, one of the outside men, yelled out,

"Sir, I found something, it looks like someone had a sweet tooth!"

When I leaned on the front porch railing and peered around the corner, I saw him coming towards me with a blue object. It was the wrapper of a Russian Troika chocolate bar. It was our first tangible evidence that we were at the right place.

"Good job, bag it and tag it."

We would later search it for prints.

We continued the search, but it was sparse pickings. We were dealing with professionals and they had done a thorough job of cleaning up. Just at the moment I had finished searching one of the upstairs bedrooms, my headset clicked and I heard Anthony, who had been searching outside say,

"Sir, you'd better come out here."

Wondering what he had found now, I descended the stairs and went out. Anthony and a couple of the guys were in the back yard, which curved up gently until it became part of the mountainside. And then I saw what had attracted their attention. They were standing around an area that was devoid of vegetation. All that could be seen was a large patch of red clay dirt. There were several rectangular depressions. We all realized that we had found what had become of the family that had lived in the big plantation house. Things had taken a drastic turn. This, more than anything else, angered me. One thing was one of our operatives being killed, at least we knew the risk when we took the job, but it was another situation entirely when an innocent family, alienated to everything that had happened, was massacred. I vowed to myself to do my utmost to get the person responsible for this.

I switched channels on my communications pack and called the San Juan office. Gina had been monitoring the channel but as per our standard operating procedures, would not contact us until the operation was over and we contacted her.

"Hello!"

"Hi, this is Gina."

"Gina, Matt here. We found the house, we broke in as we had planned, and there was no resistance. There wasn't anybody inside, friendly or otherwise. We think that we've located the family that lived in the house. At this time, we believe they were killed and buried in the back yard. We need a forensic team sent out here immediately and transport for the bodies. We've just secured the house, and we are about to finish our evidence search."

"I'm glad there wasn't any firefight. We'll send out the forensics and a couple of local police units for crowd control. I'll wait for the search results."

Then she added, "I wish I could've been there."

"I know, but someone had to be in charge of dispatching the cavalry if needed. Besides, I couldn't stand the idea of you getting hurt."

"That's precisely why the Company discourages intra-personnel relationships, it affects operational efficiency, and your sentiments get in the way of work. Our personal life should be separate from our professional life, besides, I can take care of myself, and conversely how do you think I feel when you're out there in harm's way."

That last part had slipped out inadvertently.

"How do you feel?"

"Listen, just because we broke up doesn't mean ..., forget it, I'm not going to discuss our personal relationship and have it broadcast to anyone who happens to tap in on this frequency."

I smiled.

"You know the chances of that happening are minuscule. Don't you?"

"Just the same, I'm not having that conversation now."

"O.K., but I'd like to talk about this sometime soon."

"We'll see."

After a slight pause, "We have a confirmation on the forensic team, they're on their way. I'll talk to you later."

And with that, she was out.

"Boss!"

I was bought back to the present situation. I turned around to see Stewart rushing up to me.

"You're not going to believe this one."

"Try me."

"Well the Russian fellow who escaped. He's here."

"Here?"

"Come and see."

Puzzled, I followed Stewart to the outside of the house and down a little dirt path through the woods up a sloping hillside until we reached a clearing. Our escaped Russian friend was indeed there. He was on his back, wide-open unseeing eyes to the sun, and a gaping slit in his throat that extended from ear to ear.

17

This was very bad news indeed. The Russian had been killed and someone else had the information.

I looked at Stewart who gave me a quizzical look in return.

"This is like musical chairs, who has the information now?"

"Stu, I wish I knew; I wish I knew."

After a pause I added, "I don't even know how to proceed from here. I'm at a loss."

After a moment's thought I added, "The first thing we're going to do is scour the scene and then sanitize it so that no one knows we were ever here."

The whole team started working on that and we were finished in just under three hours, with nothing else of consequence found at the scene. I called my friend, Fulgencio Jimenez, one of the governor's aides and explained the particulars of the situation.

"You're playing with the big boys now." Was his comment and he added, "So, what can I do for you?"

"Well, you know how it is, we can't be tied to this is any way. We have to become invisible."

"I see, and what do I get in return?"

PEDRO VARGAS

"My agency will not stop looking for the killers of the Crespo family which inhabited the house, and when they are found, I will call you, and you will become the heroic investigator who tracked them down and collared them."

Chuckling he replied, "That sounds very good. I know you Matt, and I trust that you will make every effort to find them."

After a short period of silence he added, "O.K., you've got it, I'll wave my magic wand and your people will become invisible."

We had done favors for each other, on and off, on an unofficial basis of course, so that we owed each other, but we really didn't keep track. I would help him any time he needed a favor, and I knew I could count on him to do the same, regardless of what favors we had done for each other in the past.

He had the scene secured by local police and true to his word, my people become invisible. To the press, and local authorities, this was just another case of unexplained violence and murder. The implications fed to the press, and which later appeared in the newspapers and television news reports were that the events probably tied in to a drug war between two rival drug gangs with the Crespo family being caught in the middle and held as innocent hostages and finally killed accidently. It was sort of close to the truth.

Meanwhile, the interrogation of the prisoners had continued at the San Juan location under Gina's direction. As I had explained before, this was more than just asking questions. Various modes of "persuasion" were used. The Soviet embassy would probably register a half-serious complaint about the treatment of their agents, but they knew better. Our agents, when captured, suffered the same treatment and worse. Officially, the prisoners were returned in fine condition, with no harm done, but in reality, they usually had to have long hospital stays, sometimes rehabilitation, and always psychological treatment. We returned the favor whenever we captured any of their agents. We both knew the stakes in the game. Nothing was said by either side in the interest of maintaining good diplomatic relations, unless things went to the extreme, such as in case of a death. Sometimes, at the risk of sounding like a male chauvinistic pig, I asked myself about the appropriateness of a woman, in this case Gina, running this type of operation. But to give her her dues, this was not the first time she had done this, and just as in the past, she handled her assignment with aplomb and in a very efficient manner.

I called her again. "Gina, anything new?" I asked.

Stewart had his men initiating the interrogation of the prisoners virtually minutes after they had been captured and had only left the scene to participate in the raid.

"I've got some information for you." Gina said. She sounded excited.

I listened expectantly.

"It seems like the man who directed this little team was an old KGB friend named Sergei Golitsin. He's the man you met at the safe house with the little problem of a slit throat. I think you've crossed paths with him before. We verified with our records and it's him. Now here's where it gets really interesting. According to Mr. Andreev, whom you may remember as the man who gave us the location of the safe house, our friend, Mr. Golitsin, ran this operation, but neglected to tell the group that this was his own little project. They were under the impression the whole time that this was a KGB operation. Dima realized it wasn't when Sergei confided in him as they went to the cave. He wanted to cut him in on the deal. It seems he needed a little help in working some of the details, and even though Mr. Andreev says he didn't approve of it, he's expressing a little concern about having to return to the KGB, and is looking for a deal to cross over to us. The information he's giving is a way of showing his goodwill to us. He's really scared."

"I don't blame him. If that story gets out, he won't have a very warm reception at KGB headquarters."

"Well we'll have to see how things turn out with him, although it looks good. He's hinted at some other information he has that we can use."

"Well, if he's not just blowing smoke, that would be very good news indeed."

"I agree, and Matt?"

"Yes."

"I've been thinking, if Sergei indeed was working alone, that would mean that the KGB didn't have an inkling about the information. It was in Sergei's interest that no copies be made, or that even the substance of the information leak out, because that would undermine his bargaining power. So it means that the information was still under wraps until now."

"Until now." I repeated, as I mulled this over.

"The big question is; who has the memos now?"

Gina replied, "We're trying to determine that now, but all of our guests deny any knowledge of having seen them or what happened to them. All they know was that they were in Mr.

Golitsin's possession at the time of the raid, and as we know, they certainly weren't there when the body was recovered. The guys that discovered the body and did the search never saw them, I asked."

"So that means that either he hid the papers in a well concealed place we haven't found yet, or, they were stolen anew."

"We're not going to through that again, are we?"

"I sincerely hope not, but the only way we will know for sure is if someone else contacts us, or the information leaks out. If it's hidden and we can't find it, all we can do is cross our fingers and hope it's never discovered, at least not in this century."

"So where do we go from here?

"Well the first thing is to repeat our search of the safe house site, with extra attention to detail, and if nothing is found, we'll just have to keep our ears to the ground and see if we hear any whispers about the memos on the street."

"Mr. Gardner hasn't called yet."

"Well miracle of miracles, I'll call him and beat him to the punch. Meanwhile, I'll take a trip out there to your locale tomorrow to review data, and regroup, and plot new strategy."

"That sounds good; at what time will you be here?"

"I'll try to make it in by nine, and then we can work until one. Maybe after that we can have lunch at the Zipperale. It's been some time since I've been there, and in the afternoon we can plan on what we're going to do with the prisoner situation."

"Are you inviting me out?"

"Just for business."

"Just a business lunch?" she asked with feigned skepticism.

"Just a business lunch." I reaffirmed solemnly.

There was a slight pause. I could tell she was weighing her options.

Abruptly she answered, "O.K.; sounds like a plan. I'll see you tomorrow then.

"See you."

As I hung up the phone I realized that I felt like a little kid on Christmas Eve. I would be seeing Gina tomorrow. But something intruded into my pleasant thoughts, and I realized I still had to call Mr. Gardner. As the saying goes, pain before pleasure.

18

I picked up the phone with great reluctance and dialed Mr. Gardner's direct line.

"Hello?"

"Hello, Mr. Gardner it's me, Matt."

"Matt! I tied up with another matter, I hadn't the opportunity to reach you, but I was expecting your call. So tell me, what's happened?"

I hope he hadn't set his hopes too high because they were about to get crushed. I told him about the information that lead to the raid on the safe house. He interrupted

"Why wasn't I told about the plans for the raid?"

"With all due respect sir, there was no time, it had be done as quickly as possible, and the planning and coordinating were done that same night, and we do have a degree of latitude in the field, don't we?."

"Well, yes," he said reluctantly, "I need assertive people out there; people who can take the initiative and that's why you're on the case."

"Thank you sir, besides that, a written report with all the details will be on your desk probably by tomorrow."

"Very well, go on then."

I took a deep breath, gathered my thoughts, and proceeded. I went on and described the raid, the lack of resistance, the discovery of the murdered family, and finally the finding of the body of Mr. Sergei Golitsin and the mystery of the papers that once again, were missing.

"Did the man commit suicide?"

"That's a good question, and the answer from the forensic team is that he appears to have been set up to look like a suicide. The knife that did him in was in his hand, a Russian Kizlyar hunting knife. It had his prints on it too. But the idea of suicide by slitting his throat seemed a bit absurd, and here's the topper. Forensics went to his record and found he was a lefty, but the wound was consistent with a right handed slasher. Also, they searched the back of the shirt he was wearing and found two fibers from what we presume was from the attacker's clothing when he was held from behind. They're being analyzed to see if we can extract any other information from them. At this point we're fairly certain it was a homicide that was posed as a suicide."

There was silence on the other side.

After several seconds I queried, "Mr. Gardner?"

He had probably come to the realization that the papers were in other hands and was momentarily stunned into silence.

"Mr. Gardner?" I ventured again.

"Yes, sorry, I was thinking on what you said."

After another pause he added, "Then we still have the same problem we had before, the papers are still missing."

"Yes sir, we had come to that same realization. Now we don't know if it's in the hands of any of our adversary countries, and if they'll make them public."

"They could be in enemy hands, and due to the nature of the material, we would hear about it soon enough or they could be in private hands, and likewise we would hear about that soon enough, but my gut instinct is that they've been destroyed or secreted away, maybe never to be found again."

"Well we've got to find out somehow."

"At this point, all we can do is wait. Only time will tell what happens."

This was a complete turnaround, I was exhorting Mr. Gardner to have the Agency take action, and he was taking everything in a laid back manner. Perhaps he was right, perhaps there was nothing we could really do until we acquired new information; if there was any new information to be acquired.

"I see your point sir. We will take an active role in keeping everyone alert to anything new on the streets, we'll tap all our contacts, in a word, and we'll follow all the usual procedures."

"I want to be immediately informed of anything new and I know you'll be doing your best. I have the utmost confidence in you Matt, and if anybody can get the information on the paper's whereabouts, I know it would be you."

"Thank you, Mr. Gardner for your confidence in me. I'll try not to let you down."

"I know you won't. We'll keep in touch"

"Will do."

With that he hung up. A much more mellow conversation than I had anticipated under the circumstances. I stood there pensive, wondering about what my next course of action should be. I decided that the best thing would be to follow Mr. Gardner's advice and wait. I felt like it was going to be a long wait. As in many other things in my life, I was wrong about this too.

19

The next day, I set off to our San Juan location for my rendezvous with Gina. I was there by eight, had some coffee, and stale Danish, and then Gina, Stewart, and the other agents that had participated in the raid, sat with me around the round table and redacted a report with everyone's point of view incorporated. After reviewing it, it was faxed to Mr. Gardner. We finished about 1:20, and after excusing myself, I set out with Gina to the Zipperale for our late lunch.

The Zipperale is a popular restaurant located in the San Juan suburb of Hato Rey. It had a German decor, and true to its Germanic name, served German dishes, but it also had a large selection of local favorites that were prepared exquisitely. It was a perfect blend of culinary influences. Our waiter, Lorenzo seated us and asked for our drink orders. I ordered a Mojito with Bacardi rum, and Gina did likewise. I had first assured myself that they used sweet spearmint leaves, and not the slightly bitter, and more common plain mint which was a little quirk I had. When my drink arrived, I sat back drinking the concoction and pretended to look at the menu while actually looking over the top of it and stealing furtive glances at Gina. She would sip, purse her lips, and concentrate on the selections. She looked absolutely adorable. I kept remind-ing myself that I had to focus on the menu. The arrival of our garlic bread momentarily interrupted my little game. Our waiter asked if we were ready to order and we decided to order a *paella marinara* for two, a delicious combination of rice, lobster, clams, and other seafood cooked to perfection. In my mind, this was the best *paella* in Puerto Rico.

After some small talk, and a small wait, our food was brought. "This is good." Gina said as she alternately sipped a fresh drink and used her fork to select a large piece of lobster from the rice with one hand. I, on my part, got caught up in looking at her as she ate. God, she looked beautiful even chewing. All of a sudden she sensed my gaze on her and looked up from her food. Looking straight up at me, she caught me and said,

"Remember, this is a business only lunch." but she smiled slightly as she said it.

"Yes ma'am, I'll keep that in mind." I answered with exagger-ated solemnity.

She looked up, caught the mischief in my eyes, and broke out laughing. It had been a while since I had seen that laugh and it felt like rain to a desert. Everything was right in my world as long as that laughter was there.

"You know, you have the most beautiful laugh in the world." I said, before I could help myself.

She looked directly into my eyes, trying to gauge the truth-fulness of my feelings when I made that statement. After a slight pause she answered softly, "Well I'm glad you like it." and then she added, "It was you who made it disappear for a long time."

"Now you're trying to send me on a guilt trip." I replied, trying to sound jocular, but the truth was, she was right and it pained me to think about it.

There was another uncomfortable moment of silence, and then I decided to take the plunge and asked, "Can I ever patch things up with you?"

She looked to the side, resting her chin on her palm. She remained like that for what seemed to me a long time, and then slowly turned to face me again, with a hurt expression on her face that I knew I was responsible for and which I hoped I could dedicate the rest of my life to erase, if I were given the chance.

She replied sadly, "Maybe."

Then looking down at her plate she added, "I'm really confused right now Matt. You know that I still love you and I always will, and that will never change, but having said that, I have this little voice in my head that asks me, can I trust him? Can I really trust him? I'd like to just answer yes and go back to the way we were, but it's not that easy. I really don't know what to do."

"I know I can repeat that you can trust me until the turn of the century and it won't mean a thing, but all I can say is that I've changed, I've really changed, and all I can do is tell you this and say I'm sincere, but only time will show you that I really mean it."

I looked at her, but she wouldn't look up. Finally after a few moments she did.

"I'll think about it. I'll take into consideration what you said. I am not going to rush into things again. Maybe..., maybe."

I was ecstatic. Maybe was infinitely better than no.

20

When we got back from lunch, as expected, we had a message from the Russian embassy. They had heard of the incident involving the "honorable" citizens of their country and they were "outraged" that these might be treated disrespectfully, and wanted these citizens released from our custody immediately and were awaiting our response. Of course, what that really meant was, that they realized they had been caught with their pants down, they suspected that we had realized we were dealing with a rogue agent, and they would prefer having him returned. I relished the situation.

I then had a reply sent stating that we indeed have two people in our custody and that we were ascertaining the veracity of their claim of Russian citizenship and once this was fully corroborated; they would then be released from custody. I added the helpful statement that if they had any documents or information to help verify their identity and these could be forwarded to us it would be very helpful in the present situation. I smiled when I thought of the position the Russian ambassador was in. He knew that we knew. He couldn't make a big stink about the situation, but he had the Soviet bosses breathing down his neck.

A very sticky situation for him. I couldn't very well turn in Dimas Andreev, he had already been compromised. If he went back, there was only a very bleak future for him. If we sent him back, it would probably mean certain death for him. His only choice was to beg for asylum, and perhaps it would be in our best interest to accommodate him, not only for himself, but as an example for other Russian agents to consider, if they would want to make the jump. Of course, nothing came free, and he would have to go through extensive questioning, and we would have to have verifiable and reliable information come from all this, but all in all, I thought this was very likely to come to fruition.

His companion, on the other hand, was a hard boiled case. He refused to talk, refused any deal, and in general was extremely uncooperative. In fact, we had separated the two for interrogation from the onset. He would probably be released and the Russians would order his return. He would know nothing about Dima Andreev's situation, and therefore could not give any information on what had happened to him. Moscow, of course, would assume the worse, as well they should, and for show, would scream through diplomatic channels for Andreev's return, but they knew they had a snowball's chance in hell of that happening.

I talked with Gina and told her to initiate the automatic diplomatic responses. We had to play the charade out. Then I instructed Stewart to offer the immunity deal and if accepted, Gina was to initiate the documentation package to make it legal. Mr. Primakov, on the other hand, was going to be declared *persona non grata,* and would have deportation papers prepared for him. I liked it when everything fell into little black or white squares and could be neatly arranged and classified. It was unfinished business like the whereabouts of the missing papers that drove me crazy.

In that regard, I thought that I would better advance the cause if I went back to the Guanica base, and created some space where I could think, so I informed Gina and Stewart that I was returning. After what had turned out to be a hard day's work, and after a bittersweet goodbye to Gina (where I had to play the role of the unimpassioned boss), I found myself on Route 2, at five in the afternoon, heading back to my little inherited hideaway on the beach. Since I had pulled everyone over to the San Juan office, I would have the place to myself.

The first thing I did when I arrived was to check for any new faxed messages. Since I hadn't received any calls on my cell, I didn't expect any, but there was always the possibility that they had wanted to send information via a secure line but as expected, there were no messages. With no new information to work on, I opened a bag of potato chips, poured myself a cold *Medalla* beer, and went out to the porch, sat on my lounger, propped my feet on the railing, and enjoyed one of God's most spectacular shows, the sunset over the Caribbean Sea. The warm sea breeze, the beer, and the reds, yellows, and oranges melded together and put me into a cozy, lethargic state of mind. It didn't get better than this. I had achieved what I wanted. I was able to clear my mind so that I could think about the facts objectively, but when I started thinking about the safe house, the dead Russian, and the call to Mr. Gardner, my thoughts strayed to my lunch with Gina, and naturally my thoughts progressed to Gina herself, and then to my unresolved feelings toward her. I got up, found an ice bucket and filled it, got some lemons, broke a seal on a new pint of *Bacardi* rum, and sat back down and prepared myself the first of a succession of drinks and sipped it at a slow pace, and watched as the sun dipped lower and lower into the horizon and everything got darker and darker, until there was nothing but black.

When I awoke, the sun was shining brightly. What had wakened me was the peripheral alarm system. Pretty soon, unless I called them off, the local police would be showing up as per the arrangement we had with them. They protected us, and we would provide help with any urgent information request they might have. I wasn't too worried about the alarm; our equipment was barricaded in a steel reinforced room, and had a security system incorporating laser beams that would frustrate even the most experienced petty thief.

I looked out to shore and saw two figures; it looked as if it were two local kids, brothers it seemed. They were about twelve and eight. As young kids were prone to do, they had disregarded the posted no entry signs and had crossed the property line walking along the shoreline. At this point, they were running along the surf, splashing water on each other, and screaming and laughing at the top of their lungs. I knew that I should stand up on the porch authoritatively and yell at them to get out, but as it was, I watched them wistfully. I wished I could be one of them. Those kids had it right, and we adults had it wrong. We should all play in the surf, enjoy life, and live only in the present. Why preoccupy ourselves with hate, greed, or envy. Ah! If only it were that easy. I realized that I was getting old. Maybe too old for this job, and that realization made me sad. That's what happens when I wake up with an early morning hangover, I get philosophical. I got up and called off the local police watchdogs.

I returned and sat back and let the early morning sun burn my eyelids. I could feel the cool breeze, hear the surf and gulls, and felt the sun's warmth. For the first time in days, I was completely relaxed. But then I started thinking about the previous day's events. There was something that bothered me at a subconscious level. I couldn't figure out what it was, and then all of a sudden, it hit me.

I called the San Juan office.

"Hello"

It was Stewart.

"Hi, it's me, Matt"

"Hello boss, I saw you were missing in action yesterday afternoon. Gina told me you had gone back."

"Yeah, I had to come over here and create some space just to hear myself think. Listen, I need you to do me a favor."

"Anything at all, shoot."

"You know the knife that was found at the scene, next to Sergei's body?"

"You mean the Kizlyar?"

"Yes, it's a custom made knife, I need you to tap your Russian contacts and see if they can get the spec sheet and see who it was made for."

I could hear a slapping sound over the phone, and I could only imagine Stewart hitting himself on the forehead.

"I should have been on top of that. I don't know how I missed it. I'll get right on it boss."

"Well you have a lot going on right now, I'm sure you would have gotten down to it eventually."

"Yeah, I guess, but I shouldn't have missed it."

"I only thought of it because of a detail I'm thinking of, if my hunch pans out, I'll tell you more."

"O.K. boss, like I said, I'm on top of it."

"Call me immediately if you get something."

"Will do."

"Talk to you later."

I hung up. I was almost certain of my hunch, actually an observation, and if it checked out, there was going to be terrible consequences, and somebody would have a lot of explaining to do.

21

The next day I was headed back to San Juan. It was hard for me to stay out of the center of action. Although the Guanica base had a basic brig system for prisoners, we actually preferred having them in San Juan. *La Fortaleza* (*The Fortress*) was actually a part of the structures built to defend the San Juan harbor between 1533 and 1540. Its original name had been *Palacio de Santa Catalina* (St. Catheline's Palace). In 1846 work was done to replace its military facade with one more becoming of a governor's residence, which was what it had become since 1822. The result was a new splendid palatial facade. It was imposing and beautiful, superbly landscaped with palm trees, and tropical fauna and overlooking the San Juan Bay. The original building had, in case it came under attack, been built with secret corridors which ran all the way to the *El Morro* fort; the idea being that in the event of an actual attack the governor could transfer in secret to the protection of the fort. Along the corridor's portion nearest to the fort, there were several antique prison cells which were hidden deep in the bowels of the earth. These antique holding cells being where we now held our Soviet guests. I wanted to ask them a couple of questions in person and observe their reactions.

When I got to the office, I was greeted by Stewart, and then taken to Gina's office, where I proceeded to inform her of my desire to interrogate the prisoners face to face. I was assigned an interpreter and we walked down San Jose street and turning down La Fortaleza street approached our secret access to the underground tunnel system. Several years ago, we had a acquired a souvenir store and used it as a front to the access of the tunnel system. I entered and said hello to Bernardo Mejias, our long time employee. He had no idea that he actually worked for the CIA. To him, I was just a generous boss, paying him a salary that was way over the current going salary. He received me on very infrequent occasions where I would exchange some pleasantries and then lock myself in the "accounting room", to do paperwork with orders not to be disturbed under any circumstance. Since he was also given generous year-end bonuses, it was unlikely that he would do anything to jeopardize his job. Indeed, he had been with us over 8 years. Of course, it didn't hurt that the store was making an incredible profit. It had been set up by one of our business section people, Al Schroeder who had a master's degree in business administration. He had picked out the right locale, business plan, and merchandise and the operation had surprisingly and unexpectedly, become a huge success. It had paid for itself within a year, and had then begun turning the aforementioned profit. Bernardo had been made the in-store manager and worked very efficiently in his role, so all in all, everyone was very happy.

After saying hello and making some small talk, I disappeared down the short corridor, into the little room in the back with the translator and shut the door. Bernardo had been instructed not to interrupt us under any circumstance whatsoever and he maintained strict compliance with this. After making sure the door was locked, I reached under the desk and pressed one of the ornate carved grape bunches on the desk's back edge and a section of wall between two thin bookcases, slid open noiselessly. The translator and I walked through. On the other side I hit a button and the door closed again. If Bernardo ever managed to open the locked office door, he would have been an extremely puzzled man.

We walked down the corridor. The black, brown and tan mottled stains against the ancient white stucco looked like continents drawn on an old cartographer's map. In spite of the modern air conditioning, there was always a stale odor in the air. In the enclosed space our footsteps resounded with an echo. Subconsciously, we walked in silence as if we had to respect the memory of those who had walked here long ago and were now gone. We walked, and after several minutes we finally arrived at the section where the cells were. One of my men, whom I recognized as a new recruit by the name of Jerry Walker stood up from the array of closed circuit camera displays to greet us. He had probably followed our progress from the minute we had entered the corridor system. With a push of a button he could have a half dozen men down here in an instant. Jerry himself was monitored back at the office. The new recruits worked down here in twelve hour stints. I didn't envy their job. Of course, they were paid very well, which in turn, bred loyalty.

"Good morning Mr. Hines."

"Good morning, having an eventful day so far?"

"Besides the food crew, you're the first people I've seen all day."

I smiled in sympathy.

"We're here to talk to the house guests."

"Yes sir, your passes please."

I was glad he hadn't been intimidated by who I was and had asked for our passes. If he hadn't done so, he'd probably be looking for a new job tomorrow. We had to abide by strict protocol, and I had to produce my ID badge which was inserted into the slot in a machine by his side which promptly spit it out the other side while a green light turned on, giving me clearance, and the same with my companion. I saw our photo ID and pertinent data come up on his computer screens.

"Everything's kosher, come on in."

He punched in a number on his keyboard and a steel bar gate slid open behind him. We thanked him and went in. There were six cells. Each with a rudimentary toilet and bunk bed, and illuminated by fluorescent lighting. There was a TV in each cell, after all, we weren't animals. Two of the cells were occupied by our new "guests".

Both of them were in identical positions, laying on their bunks with their hands behind their heads looking up at the TV. One of them sat up when we came in, and the other just gave us an insolent look and remained as he was. I talked as the translator made them know what I was saying.

"Good afternoon gents. I see you're both enjoying the luxuries of our hospitality."

They both game me sullen looks. After a moment, I continued.

"Well it seems that your luck is going to change. Your people have been asking for you and we may be persuaded to let you go.

Of course, during your stay here you have become very popular and an object of interest to your former comrades."

I could see a tiny glimmer of interest begin to form in their expressions.

"Before I let you go, I have to ask you a couple of questions and if you answer, this whole process can be expedited. So I'll start with the gentleman in cell four."

The prisoner I had called for was the one who had sat up on his bunk when we came in, Andreev, the one who had concerns about being returned to Russia. His body language gave evidence that he would be the more receptive of the two to questioning. His cell was opened, and a guard who had been called over from the main office stood with a Colt 45 watching over him. I motioned for him to sit at a small interrogation room we had fashioned in an adjoining cell. It had the requisite two way mirrored glass to shield observers in a cubicle that harbored all sorts of recording equipment. Stewart had previously gone in and was manning the recorders. I had requested that I be the one to do interrogation this time.

"Smoke?" I asked.

The Russian didn't look up; he was gazing down at the table. I placed a pack of Kools on the table and slid it towards him. It stopped right under his down turned eyes. He looked at it for a couple of seconds then slowly picked it up and opened the pack. I threw a book of matches and he lit up and took a puff and blew a blue cloud towards the ceiling.

"You know, you're in deep shit here." I wondered vaguely how the translator handled that.

"If we hand you back, your bosses are not going to be very happy with you. They'll think you were all in on this. That you were going to take a split and run."

A violent outburst followed and I gathered from the translation, that the Russian was vehemently denying any knowledge of acting outside of what he thought was a KGB operation.

"Well, I'm just telling you what the perception of your people is and in this instance perception is reality. I'm sure you have to agree that will be the likely scenario."

I let that sink in before proceeding.

"I know you are interested in staying in this country, and I can make that happen. You have given us some information we needed and we appreciate it. If you are willing to clarify a few other things maybe I can make arrangements so that you can stay. We can give you another identity and even establish you in an American town with a large Russian population. No one could ever find you. You would even get a monthly stipend."

I waited as this was translated.

"What I'm going to do right now, is to leave the room, let you think about it, and I'll be back in half an hour."

I left the cell and raided Jerry's coffee machine and stole a couple of his doughnuts. The translator shared them with me. I would make sure to send down a fresh box for the guard later on. We munched in silence for a while; then discussed the local baseball championship that was going on between the Arecibo *Lobos* and the Ponce *Leones*. After a half hour had passed, we both got up and went back to Andreev's cell.

He was slouched over the table with his arms over his head. When he saw heard us come in he stood up straight.

"What do you wish to know?"

I thrilled to hear that and immediately started questioning him before he changed his mind. There were basically two areas I wanted information on, and I delved into the first one.

"Who killed the Crespo family?"

With some reluctance, and after assuring him that the interrogation cell was soundproofed and nothing could be heard from outside, he confessed that the killer was the companion we had imprisoned in the other cell. His name, according to Andreev, was Andros Primakov, but he was known in the KGB as the "Mad Bear", due to his psychotic behavior. He was extremely unstable, but was kept active and in the field because of his proficiency in killing, and he didn't particularly care who the target was. He seemed to have no conscience and would kill indiscriminately.

"Who gave the instructions to kill the family?

That had been Sergei, the one who later had died with his throat slit. He gave Primakov the order shortly after they had broken into the home. All four members had been blindfolded, tied, and gagged, then marched outside and made to kneel. "Mad Dog" Primakov came silently behind each one and savagely slit their throat. As the last one lay gasping for air bleeding to death, the rest of the group, including Andreev, were called outside to help dig the graves. As they worked Primakov delighted himself in the recounting of all the grisly details. Having satisfied myself that he seemed to be telling the truth on this point, I proceeded to the next area of questioning.

I asked if he knew who had killed Sergei. He didn't know. Having escaped from the caverns, he had arrived back at the safe house alone. He and "Mad Bear" Primakov had been taken into custody by our team, and the rest had been killed in the firefight and by the tram "accident", so he was as puzzled as we were as to how Sergei had met his death. I finished up with questions on if he was aware if Sergei had made any negotiation or come into contact with anyone locally. Dimas Andreev was unaware of any such communication.

I thanked Andreev for his cooperation. We got up, and I assured him that I would start to process his paperwork and coordinate with Immigration, Justice, and State Departments, to obtain a new identity and expedite U.S. citizenship for him. After returning him to his cell we proceeded to call out Mr. Andros Primakov. With the knowledge we now had, of who he was, we first made sure that he backed up to the bars and put his hands through an opening for this purpose. He was handcuffed and instructed to lie face down on the bunk bed. I then proceeded in with caution, accompanied by Mr. Walker, the guard, who held a taser gun at the ready. I proceeded to put leg shackles on the prisoner and then ran a chain from the handcuff to the leg shackles. He was then marched into the interrogation room. I didn't expect any information from him, and I wasn't disappointed. He refused to answer any questions and his only gesture was to demand seeing a consulate official. I had expected as much, and had only gone through the motions only to throw suspicion off Andreev. If we hadn't made an attempt to interrogate him he would have wondered why and then it would have dawned on him that maybe Andreev had spilled the goods. After a couple of questions and a few threats thrown in for show I ended the interview with him and he was marched back to his cell. Even though it killed me, because of his diplomatic immunity, I would have to start the extradition process for the "Mad Bear". He would have to be returned to his own country.

22

When Gina heard about 'Mad Bear' Primakov's involvement in the killing of the Crespo family, she felt morally obligated to personally inform the family members of the new development. I didn't entirely agree, feeling that it was a local police matter, but I told her that if she was going to go, I would be willing to accompany her. There were two other brothers in the family. One was Carlos, a local radiologist with several offices in the metro area, and the other brother was Richard, apparently the black sheep of the family. He had been in jail for various offenses such as assault and battery, narcotics trafficking, etc. He was at present, without a permanent address. We decided to visit Carlos and a half hour later we found ourselves, motoring down A-52 towards Montehiedra, an exclusive development, just outside of the San Juan metro area where Carlos, the eldest son and one of the two survivors of the Crespo family lived. Arriving at the house on Falcon Street, we parked and went up the elegantly landscaped walkway and rang the bell.

A young Hispanic male opened the door.

"Carlos Crespo?" I asked in Spanish.

"Yes", he replied, eyeing us warily.

"We are from a government agency doing an investigation in an incident in which your name came up and we have some information that we have to make you aware of. May we come in for a few minutes?"

He looked a little confused and wary of us.

"What's this about? Let me see your I.D.'s"

We diligently took out our I.D's and showed them to him. He still looked a little suspicious of us, but invited us in. We sat on a leather couch next to each other facing him. What I took to be his wife entered with a little boy who seemed to be about three.

"Carlos?"

"Honey, it's all right, these men are from the government, and they're here to get some information."

We looked at each other. There was not going to be any easy way to do this. I looked at Carlos and then I addressed him.

"Mr. Crespo, are you the son of Mr. Eusebio Crespo?"

"Yes."

I could see fear entering his eyes, as if he anticipated what I was going to say.

"He has a small farm near Dos Bocas?"

"Yes."

My heart was racing now, and I knew Carlos had to be in the same state.

"I'm afraid I have some bad news to give you."

The wife had silently come to the love seat where Carlos was and had sat down beside him, with her son on her lap and instinctively put her arm around him.

"There was an incident on the farm, and there's no good way to say this but I'm afraid you parents and sister and brother were killed."

"Nooooo!" The word was bellowed out by Carlos as he covered his face in anguish and sank to his knees on the floor. His body was racked by sobbing. His wife pressed her face against his back and with tears streaming down her face, called his name while automatically still holding the child who also started crying.

"Carlos! Carlos!"

Gina and I also stood up and knelt beside him.

"It's all right. It's all right." I said over and over again as I patted him, the falsest words I had ever said.

After a long time, the sobbing decreased, and between his wife and I, we lifted him back onto the love seat.

After a long while, and an awkward wait, Carlos finally again acknowledged our presence and turning to me with tears streaming down his face and an anguished look on his face asked,

"What happened?"

"Well most of this is government information that I can't disclose. But I can tell you in general."

"What HAPPENED?" he asked in a stronger voice as he looked directly into my eyes.

I decided to tell him the truth as far as I could.

"A group of Russians were trying to develop an operation on the island and needed a base of operations, and decided that your family's homestead would be the place; maybe because it was isolated. We are just starting the investigation. We think only one man was responsible for the deaths of your family."

"Who is he?"

"It's a name that would mean nothing to you."

"Who IS HE?"

"His name is Andros Primakov."

"What are they going to do with him?"

Before I answered, I glanced at Gina, for moral support. This was extremely hard.'

"Well, that's the difficult part Carlos. We can't do anything, as a foreign diplomatic agent, he has immunity. We are having him declared *persona non grata* and he will be deported back to his country."

"WHAT? nothing is going to be done? He is going to get away with murder?"

"I'm sorry, but that's the way it is. Because of diplomatic immunity, nothing can be done."

I couldn't look him in the eyes as I said this. He buried his face in his hands again.

"Arraignment for deportation will be tomorrow." I continued in a soft voice, "We want him out of here as soon as possible."

"Where are they?"

"Your parents and brother and sister are at the Arecibo Regional Hospital morgue." I handed him a card.

"We will consider it our duty to help with the funeral expenses, in fact, most of it will be covered. Please give us a call to arrange the details."

We stood up. "We are very sorry. We really mean that."

"I also have to go to the farm."

"Right now, as you can imagine, we are processing the farm for forensic evidence, and we will not be done for at least another day. I will contact you as soon as we can, as to when you can come."

"When will this man be in court? I want to at least see him and have him see me before he leaves."

"Well we have a hearing scheduled for 11:30 am, but maybe it's not a good idea for you to go, you'll just be frustrated."

He looked at me again. "I have to go. I have to see him."

"As I said, I don't think it's a good idea but if you insist there's nothing that I can to prevent you from being there. I'll see you tomorrow; I also have to be there."

Gina expressed her condolences and we started to leave.

"If there's anything you need or any question you have please do not hesitate to give me a call."

I went to the car and drove back in silence. I felt like a clod.

23

The next morning, dressed in my best grey suit and red tie, I drove down to the Hato Rey (a suburb of San Juan) district court to be present at the accelerated deportation proceedings for Mr. "Mad Dog" Primakov. Stewart, Gina, and some of the others were already there when I arrived. Mr. Primakov appeared with two members of the Soviet embassy and couple of bodyguards. He had apparently been brought a new change of clothes and looked downright flashy in a tan checkered sports blazer, a pale yellow silk shirt, white pants, and leather moccasins, sans socks. The judge, shuffled through the papers, it was basically a sham proceeding and everyone involved knew it, but we had to go through the official motions. It was over in less than 20 minutes. I hated the smile on Mr. Primakov's face as they took off the cuffs and he was officially handed over into his fellow countrymen's hands. He had the audacity to glance over at me specifically and smile as the cuffs were coming off. There was a group of about twelve of them, including, lawyers, his embassy people, and what seemed to be one of his local romantic interests.

We gathered our papers, briefcases, and other belongings, and found ourselves following them out on the steps. I was momentarily blinded by the bright sun. Then I looked and saw two black limousines gliding towards us and then stopping to pick up the Soviet group. They were going to ride out in style. Someone opened the door for Primakov. He stopped before entering and looked up at our group and smiled once again. All of a sudden, I saw a crimson spot appear on his left temple, and his head jerked back. Blood started spurting out of his nose, and he seemed to freeze for a moment. Then the retort of a shot was heard. In less than a second a second crimson circle appeared on his chest, and he started falling. The noise of the second shot was heard just as his head hit the sidewalk.

In spite of our training, we were all momentarily frozen. As soon as I realized what had happened, I ran at a crouch to the limousine door, taking out my automatic as I did so, and knelt beside the dying man. I then peered out in the direction of where I had heard the shots come from. There was nothing to be seen, nor did any more shots ring out. I really didn't expect any more. I figured that the objective of the shooter had been achieved and at that moment was making his getaway. I looked at the dying man. There was nothing that could be done for him. There was screaming and hysteria from the others around him. I tried to tell them that he was beyond help, but no one listened and I finally gave up. As I started walking back to my group, I heard the pulsating siren of an approaching ambulance. Police cars arrived on the scene and some took off in the direction of where the shots seemed to have come from. I knew it would be in vain.

Carlos, one of the two surviving members of the Crespo family, had shown up at the proceedings and had been sitting at the back of the court auditorium. All of a sudden, he was standing near me as we observed the pandemonium.

"Too bad." he said.

I turned and looked at him.

"That was such a pretty shirt he had." he said as he gave me a slight smile. And he turned away and disappeared amongst the gathering crowd. And at that moment I knew.

An investigation was later initiated with no real results. A shell casing was found, the only piece of evidence recovered, and even this meager bit was 'misplaced' in the evidence room at the local police station and never again found. The investigation came to a standstill and the murder became a cold case. Carlos was called once for an interview we tried to ascertain whether he had any knowledge of the case. Of course, he claimed he didn't know anything. He had been at the court proceedings the whole time. I didn't know how, but I knew he had managed to sneak out without having been seen or missed. Even I had seen him. He smiled at me as he left the interrogation room. He had come to the questioning session wearing a pale yellow silk shirt.

24

My next task was to concentrate on the scant leads that we had gathered at the Crespo family farm, the yellow threads, and the customized hunting knife. Gina had sent the threads we had found at the scene of the safe house for analysis to our fiber analysis department. They determined that the fibers were cotton fibers, and that they were actually Scottish cotton. From the curled pattern of the second thread it was determined that this had been embroidery that was common to a *guayabera* shirt. The *guayabera* shirt was a type of shirt that was used widely throughout Latin countries especially in the Caribbean. Its origin was disputed, with the general belief that it originated either in Cuba or Mexico. The stories of how it was conceived usually involved a land owner wanting a comfortable shirt with lots of pockets to carry all his personal items such as smoking pipes, pencils, papers, etc. Be it as it may, the shirt has evolved into a design that is used widely in the Caribbean, and Latin countries. This type of this shirt is fairly long and worn on the outside of the belt line. It has a row of buttons down the front and four pockets, two up on the chest level, and two on a lower level falling over the general area of the trouser packets. They are decorated with lines of elaborate decorative embroidery running down the front. They are usually made of cotton or linen. They can be very simple and mass manufactured, or they can be very elaborate running into the hundreds of dollars. They are sometimes used in the Caribbean as an perfectly acceptable substitute for a formal suit. Indeed local government dignitaries used them in official state functions.

Being the case that the particular threads in this case, had been determined to be Scottish linen, this narrowed the field somewhat, as this higher priced fabric is used only in the more exclusive type of garments. Another unique feature of these threads were their color. Taken alone this would not be much of a clue, but combined with the knowledge of the use of the rare fabric, and what type of garment was made with it gave us a very valuable clue. It seemed that certain exclusive shops could ask for a particular hue to distinguish their product. This hue would be used only for that particular client, and was not reproduced for anyone else. That was the case in point in our situation. After contacting the manufacturer, we learned that the particular hue of yellow had been made for a shop in Miami. It was a shop called *El Palacio de la Guayabera* on Miami's famous Calle Ocho. It was owned by Cuban designer Silverio Pujols who hand designed pieces for his clientele, as individualized as any *haute couture* designers wares. He usually used English linen, or Scottish cotton for his designs, and his *guayaberas* were widely sought after, and his clients were, diverse ranging from businessmen in the higher Latin circles, movie actors, and even American presidents traveling to Mexico or the Caribbean, who wanted then for personal use, or as diplomatic gifts.

Now we had to try to locate the purchaser, not an easy task, when thousands of these were sold world-wide every year. We did have an advantage of having narrowed the point of purchase to this one exclusive store, but even that still implied a large pool of customers. I instructed Gina to send someone down to the Miami store to interview Mr. Pujols, the owner, and see what they could find out.

In the meantime, I started work on the knife. We didn't have direct access to the Soviet factory, and previous experience had shown that it was futile for our agency to obtain even the most innocuous bit of information from them. We were in luck though, one of our Soviet controllers had a contact in place at that very factory, and although she was a bit player, she had been maintained on our payroll because of her outstanding ability to become friendly with almost anyone in a very short period of time. As I was soon to find out, she would prove her worth very shortly.

The contact was asked if she had access to the records room and she did not, but, she stated, the married head of the records department had been very flirtatious with her on several occasions. She was sure she could develop that to obtain the information we needed. She was offered 4 pairs of Versace jeans, and a vacation in Svetlogorsk for two, a Baltic Sea resort town, as an incentive to come up with the information. Each pair of jeans represented a month of her salary, so that she could sell three pair and still keep one and be very economically remunerated, to say nothing of the resort vacation, so she was very motivated. Within three days she was having her lunch with the department supervisor at his desk. Two days after that she informed us that she had access to the files and was just waiting for a good opportunity to obtain the invoice records we needed.

25

Things were starting to come together. Just little bits and pieces of information, with nothing definitive, but by linking something from one source with something from another source, we could develop some direction, get closer to our missing mystery person who had killed Sergei. I worked to piece together what we had.

First of all, from the interview with Mr. Pujols, the owner of the *guayabera* store in Miami, we had learned that he was a meticulous record keeper. He had records for the computerized transactions for the last eighteen years, and had actual paper sales slips and records for several years before that and was willing to let us copy the computer disc files, and if needed, we could access the paper files. The people who had ordered a *guayabera* in Scottish cotton, and in that particular color, numbered in the hundreds on the computer records, and who knew how many in the paper slips. I decided that we would deal with the computerized information, and research the paper files if needed. It was unlikely that whoever had worn the *guayabera* at the murder scene, had worn a shirt that was older than eighteen years.

Having the name list for the *guayabera* shirt, my next logical step was to check the name on the knife invoice, which we had obtained through our factory operative, against the shirt list and see if we came up with a match. In the case of the knife, we were in a little bit of luck. It seems that the Kizlyar Company had not started making custom built knives until 1992. The search had been slightly easier as there had been fewer records to wade through.

Our contact had been given a story to feed her department supervisor boyfriend, stating that her brother was an avid fan of the company's product, and working at the Rinaldi Premier hotel in St. Petersburg, had been given one of the knives for safekeeping in the hotel's house safe. He had so admired the knife that he had copied the serial number in the hopes that someday he might be able to afford one. She convinced him to allow her to take a peek at the order to see what it would cost to duplicate. The supervisor had led her to a file cabinet and pulled the order, where it was ascertained that the employee cost was 32,870 rubles ($1,220 US), a cost which our contact said was too prohibitive for her, at which the supervisor predictively hinted that for certain favors from our operative, he could probably have the knife made at a considerable discount and maybe even bear with a major portion of the cost. Our girl just smiled at him and said she would think about it.

Later, at her lunch break, she met with her supervisor outside, and after a little conversation, said in a coy manner that she had to use the restroom. She quickly went to the department's files, located the filing cabinet, extracted the order, made a copy of it, and replacing the original back in its place, folded the copy, and placed it in her purse, and returned to her outdoor rendezvous with her supervisor. A day after that, she told her controller that she had a copy of the invoice record we needed.

The next weekend, our man, arrived at Mahachkala, the nearest airport to Kizlyar, the military airport at Kizlyar having been closed since 1991. He didn't rent a car because of the roadblocks at each town with AK-47 toting corrupt police, and because of the equally dangerous fact that drivers in Dagestan drove like reckless kamikaze pilots. He preferred taking the train. He dressed in the current fashion of a blue colored T-shirt, blue jeans held in place by a belt with a large silver eagle buckle, and a light jacket. The people in Kizlyar were very wary of strangers and a stare could be a provocation to a fight. He wanted to fit in as much as possible and not attract undue attention. He arrived carrying a large paper shopping bag and went to the *Golden Café* on the outskirts of town near a wooded area. He sat at one of the counter seats carefully placing the shopping bag on the floor next to the empty stool beside him. A few minutes later and as per instructions, the Russian factory worker carrying a large manila envelope and a purse came and sat beside him without acknowledging his presence. She placed the envelope on the counter and ordered *shashlik*, a local favorite of spiced mutton with sliced onions soaked in vinegar, accompanied by hot tea. After finishing her *shashlik* and tea she picked up her purse, paid, then bent and picked up the shopping bag and left. Our man folded the paper he was reading and placed it over the manila envelope. He then took out his wallet and paid for his coffee, and before he left he picked up the paper and the envelope and left. The switch had been made. The factory worker had her jeans and the vacation reservation, and we had our invoice copy for the special order knife.

The invoice was faxed to me and I rapidly perused it as soon as it came across. Our knife had been manufactured for a Mr. Robert Santini, living in Annandale, just outside of Washington, D.C. It seemed that that Mr. Santini, was an exporter who did heavy business in Soviet trade. A background check had no surprises, no criminal record, with the exception of a couple of DUI arrests which were almost the norm for business residents of the Capitol area. His finances showed he was well off, but there were no recent large bank deposits, and there was nothing out of the ordinary, just your regular capitalist American company.

At just about this time I received a call from Mr. Gardner regarding the progress of the investigation. I told him what we had so far, and a general idea of what we were going to do next.

"Damn it Matt!", he said, "I expect to be kept informed on the progress of this case, I have a lot on my plate and I can't keep calling you every time to see where we stand."

"I'm sorry sir, but as you see, I also have a lot of work, and I sometimes can't report as frequently as I'd like, but I do give you any important development as soon as it happens."

"Well that's just not good enough. As I told you before, this is a very important operation for me, it involves our national security, I want a daily briefing sent to me, I want to know what's happening at all times, do you understand?"

"Yes sir and I'll instruct Gina to have a daily brief prepared and sent to you. I did not mean to leave you out of the loop. I just figured that with all the work you have, you just wanted to know when anything of major interest developed."

"This is very important to me and I want to know everything that happens no matter how small it may seem. Is that clear?"

"Yes sir and any development will be passed on to you as soon as it happens."

"Very well"

With that he hung up. I felt like a four year old that had just been chastised by his father.

I concentrated on the things that had to be done, and in co-ordination with our central office in Langley, I had an around the clock surveillance mounted on Santini for ten days. After nothing unusual being noted after this amount of time, I decided to pull him in for questioning. But just before the day I was going to fly in to a CIA office in Washington, to personally interrogate him, an extraordinary thing happened.

26

On the last night of the surveillance on the Santini house, the graveyard shift, I had two operatives working in tandem. Although they were glad to be on their last watch on this particular subject, they were nonetheless, professionals, and did not relax their vigilance until the end of their shift. This was lucky for Santini, because at 3 in the morning, one of the men saw a glint from around the hedge area next to the Santini household. He lifted the lever to straighten his seat and looked closer. He didn't see anything at first, but he stayed focused on the particular spot, and after several minutes, he saw an almost imperceptible shift. Finally he was able to make out a figure in black camouflage. He poked his partner and in the same movement opened the car door and started running towards a tree, close to the Santini home for cover. The blackness of the night was interrupted by two muzzle flashes and our man heard a thump in the tree and then another bullet deflect off the side of the tree trunk he was behind. He heard it buzz off into the night with an angry bee noise, as he pulled his gun. All of a sudden, he heard three loud retorts from his left. His companion, having gone unnoticed behind the car, had been able to reach for his gun first, and had managed to squeeze off the three shots which apparently caught the would-be intruder and knocked him flat on the ground.

Both men approached the prone figure slowly, with their guns extended and at a crouch, at the same time looking out for any accomplices. By this time, the lights in the Santini house were turned on, as were the lights in several of the neighboring homes. The men ascertained that the night visitor was dead, and then called in for a containment team. Already they heard the approaching sirens of the local police. They looked at their target. He was dressed in black ninja type clothing. He was carrying a bag that later was discovered to have a few burglary implements, such as rope, a small flashlight, jiggler keys, etc. This had been his downfall, because although the bag was black, the carrying strap was held into place by two small silver clasps which glinted with the light of the street lamps.

After the arrival of the police and after everything was discreetly sorted out with our men, we had talked with Santini and we had him come in for questioning the next day. We started the session by asking if he knew why someone would try to kill him. He expressed complete surprise and didn't know of anyone who would do something like this. We asked about any underhanded or obscure deals with his exporting company. Again, he denied any such transactions, and our previous scrutiny of his bank records, finances, and business records had not shown anything out of the ordinary. We decided to change tact and hit him with the big question.

"Mr. Santini, as a representative of Soviet imports, have you ever dealt with the Kilzyar knife company?"

"Yes I have, I've had several clients that special order their products through me. In fact, I had a custom made knife crafted for myself."

"Indeed. What kind of knife was it.?"

"Well it had the head of a boar, crafted in silver, with the eyes being two small emeralds, and the rest of the hilt carved out of elk bone, and the blade was Damascus steel with decorative engraving all over it. It was very pretty and unique."

I felt tension building up in me as I built up to the next question."

"Where is that knife now?"

"Why? Did you guys find it?"

"Find it?"

"Yeah, It was stolen a couple of weeks ago."

I looked at Daniel Rogers, my interrogation partner. He had the same perplexed expression I must have had.

"Did you report it to the police?"

"Yes, they came over but didn't find any prints or anything. They made a report."

"Where did this take place?"

"At my home. My wife and I were out for the weekend, and when we came back we found the back door had been forced open. I always close all the doors in my house before I leave. Well, when I came in I noticed the door to my study was open and I realized it must of been a break-in so I told my wife not to touch any-thing, and we went to our neighbor's house and called the police from there. They found our alarm system had been disabled, and of course, the door had been forced open."

"What did they take?"

"Believe it or not, all they took was the knife."

I would verify that there was a police report, but if there was, and I had no reason to doubt it, this was a dead end road.

We thanked Mr. Santini for agreeing to come in and being interviewed. I was accompanying him to the door when he said,

"Say hello to Mr. Gardner for me."

I looked at him with surprise.

"You know Mr. Gardner?"

"Yes I do. A couple of months back, he needed a Russian translator at the spur of the moment. One of his secretaries used to be my secretary, and she mentioned that I was fluent in Russian and they contacted me, and I was able to help."

I stood there digesting this bit of information.

Mr. Santini stood there looking at me.

"Small world isn't it."

"Yes it is. It sure is."

27

I had sent for the report on the burglary at Mr. Santini's house. Mr. Santini had been right in all aspects of the incident except one. The report mentioned that there had been evidence found. They had lifted a partial print from the wireless transmitter box that was part of the burglar alarm. This sat atop a concrete light pole in front of Santini's house. It had been shot at several times with a BB gun to disable it. The several impacts had apparently broken the lid and it had fallen to the ground. Apparently the shooter picked up one of the larger pieces and chucked into a vacant lot, so it wouldn't be seen from the street, but he forgot to use his gloves for this. An investigating police officer had almost stepped on it, as he was giving a cursory look at the box to satisfy his curiosity as to how the alarm had been disabled. The print had been found by a fortunate accident. I sent it to the forensic section to see if there was any match.

Meanwhile, in Miami, Gina had compiled a list of the *guayabera* buyers and ordered a background check on all purchasers. There were over 800 names of this particular color of *guayabera* at this store. There were over a hundred who were deceased at the time of the killing of the Soviet agent, but that still left hundreds to go through. After the third day, Gina called me to keep me updated.

"We've completed a preliminary check on the entire list. We've got a lot of misdemeanors, some drugs, and two manslaughters, but the manslaughters were in jail at the time of the killing."

"It's more than probable than the man we're looking isn't on that list. Perhaps he doesn't have a criminal record, or the shirt could have been given to him as a gift, but no matter the circumstances, we know the shirt came from this store."

"We'll keep digging, and try to separate some probable suspects and then, if we have to, we can give the most likely ones a field interview to try and check out where they were on that date."

"Hopefully it won't get to that point but we'll see."

I told her to keep me informed and that I would keep on working on the evidence on my end, and that we would meet at the San Juan office later on to see what we had. She told me she was flying in from Miami that very afternoon, and we decided to meet as soon as I could.

I then received a very interesting call from the prints section. Our man there, Kevin Douglas, called me up and after the usual preliminaries told me about an unusual discovery involving the prints.

"We got a positive hit on that partial from when Mr. Santini's knife was stolen. It seems to belong to an individual named Georgio Marole, who lives in Woodbridge, a town in Virginia, just outside of Washington."

"Well I'll have someone go to interview him as soon as possible."

"I'm afraid that's going to be impossible."

"Why?"

"It seems that those prints are a match for the gentleman who was killed at the Santini home yesterday."

"You mean to tell me, that the person who broke into Santini's home to steal a knife some weeks ago is the same person who was killed at his house last night?"

"Yes."

I sat there thinking about this. Why would someone who only stole a knife come back again to the same house, and then shoot at the police, instead of just giving up. It didn't make sense.

"Sir?"

"I'm still here. I was just thinking of what you said. It doesn't make sense. Anyway, thanks for the information, and please fax me a written report as soon as you can."

"It's already written up. I'll fax it to you right now."

"Well once again thanks, and I'll call you if I need to clarify anything."

"Anything I can help you with. Bye."

I sat there mulling over that latest bit of information and meditated on what I had to do next. What I ended up doing was something I was getting very good at, I waited.

After an hour, I received the fax I had been waiting for in regard to the records of one Georgio Marole who had been killed trying to enter Mr. Santini's home presumably to kill him. I perused the records and then sat there as if struck on the head by a sledge hammer. There was one tiny fact that they had neglected to tell. It seems that Mr. Marole had been employed at times by the CIA.

I immediately called Kevin.

"You receive the records OK?"

"I sure did, but there's a small fact that you neglected to mention, he was employed by the Company!", I screamed at him.

There was a small period of silence and then,

"I thought you knew, I thought that's why you wanted the records."

His unspoken thought was that he thought I wanted to have the records "expunged" to eliminate any connection between Marole and us.

"Listen, I'm sorry. I appreciate that you got the information and faxed it over so quickly."

"It's OK. In fact as soon as I faxed you the information, I received an order from the powers from above to send them the original file and to eliminate any references to it."

"What?"

"Just what you just heard. The file doesn't exist anymore officially. You now have the one and only copy. It was an executive order bought in by personal courier. The courier took everything in the file and left."

"Did you get an ID?

"Yeah," I heard some papers rustling, "It was a Steven Winestock, ID No 12834"

"OK, I'll look into it. Thanks."

"No problem."

I was anxious to see who could be so interested in the file. I entered the information in the personnel search base and after a few seconds I sat there looking dumbly at the results. It seemed that the courier in question, Mr. Winestock, had died in an automobile accident some three months previous.

28

I sat with my feet propped on railing of the porch at the Guanica bay base house. The sun was setting, painting a spectacular vision of reds, yellows, and oranges in the sky and ocean. The cool ocean breeze blowing inland, and the *Medalla* beer helped relax me as I tried to comprehend the events that had transpired and put everything into perspective and try to make some sense of it all. First of all, we had the case where Sergei Golitsin, the Russian who had obtained the memos, and had been behind Gina's kidnapping, had been found dead at the house that the Russians had appropriated. The knife that was used, far from being one of his cohorts weapons, turned out to be made for Mr.Santini, an importer of Russian goods, who had been used by the CIA at times, as a translator-liaison agent, who later had the knife stolen from his home. The thief had left a print which later matched the prints of the person who had returned to apparently try to assassinate Mr. Santini. The would-be assassin had been identified as Mr. Georgio Marole, who, surprise, surprise, had been utilized by the Company also. Something smelled very fishy, and it wasn't the ocean I was staring at.

Suddenly a mosquito bit me and I jumped with a start in a reflexive action and turned to swat at it. Suddenly I saw splinters jump from the wood wall behind me and instantaneously a gaping hole appeared. By the time I heard the retorts from the shot, my training had taken over and I was rolling on the porch floor and crawling towards the hatch.

When I had first visited Bob, many years ago, at his beach hideaway, I noticed a large metallic commercial cooler on the front porch. I had opened it expecting to get a cool beer or soft drink, and had noticed, to my surprise, that it was completely empty. I had turned to him in surprise and saw him chuckling at my quizzical look.

"Nothing in there Matt."

"Then why do you have this here?"

"Because of this."

He had then come over to where I was standing and stuck his hand under a crack in the wood floor and had lifted up the hatch. The hatch door itself followed the irregular pattern of the floor boards so that when it was closed it was virtually impossible to detect. It also had two brackets with clamps on the underside so that a concrete slab that had been prepared for the purpose could be slid into it and clamped down. The purpose was twofold, one was that the weight would help in keeping the hatch down, and make it more difficult to open, and two, it helped in making detection more difficult because it would not sound hollow when tapped. As an extra precaution, there were four bolt latches, one on each side of the hatch, so that even if the hatch *was* detected, this, in combination with the concrete slab would make it almost impossible to open. Bob had assured me solemnly, on that day that

I was the only person, besides himself, who knew about the escape hatch, and he made me swear that I would not divulge its existence to anyone else.

"You never know who you can trust." He had said on that day.

Apparently, without words, he was implying that he trusted me.

Even after he died, I still kept my promise, not because of a sense of loyalty but because I really hadn't thought about it, and there really wasn't anybody I would want to tell anyway.

I now took the time to fasten the latches on each side and then slid the concrete slab into the brackets and clamped it into place. I could hear the zinging of bullets as they ricocheted off the porch and house. My heart was pounding as I hastened down the dark corridor towards the exit. Bob had constructed a tunnel that ran several hundred yards and that exited into a clump of sea grapes and several palms and was at an angle to the house so that I could get a good view of it. I ran the length of the tunnel as fast as I could. I exited into the vegetation and cautiously looked back out.

I could make out a black SUV, which looked like a Suburban. I was too far away to make out the tag. After several seconds of observation, I made out three men all wearing black hoods, one on each side of the house. There was probably another on the back side of the house but I couldn't see him from my vantage point. I could see the one that seemed to be the team leader signaling for the others to lay low and hold their fire.

They would probably wait for noises then fire another volley and after a while they would realize that there was no return fire. After that they would wait a while, and then they would determine that they would have to bite the bullet and come in, probably in a coordinated attack from all sides. After coming in and quickly realizing I wasn't there they would begin a search to see how I got out. I was confident that the escape door was virtually undetectable with the limited search time they would have because in the back of their mind, they had to be thinking that someone might have heard the shots and called the police.

This meant I probably had about fifteen minutes and that I better make good use of them. I walked backwards to the shore keeping the house in view at all times. Reaching another clump of sea grapes I stepped into a light wood boat that Matt had hidden there. I pushed off with oars and then once some distance away I turned on the small electric motor which operated with a barely discernible hum, and proceeded to the Guayanilla shoreline further west. The boat had been painted the same shade of blue as the sea and I crouched low in it to avoid detection. My biggest concern was that I would be run over by a larger boat or a wave runner, but I reached the Guayanilla shore without a problem.

Once there, I located a square dilapidated concrete structure almost hidden by weeds. I crouched at the base of the garage door and lifted a metal square under a rock (you had to know where to look), and uncovered a numerical touch pad. I punched in a code and the garage door opened. Inside was a beige '95 Toyota Camry courtesy, once again, of Bob's foresight. Bob had chosen the Camry because it was one of the most popular cars on the island, there were hundreds of them in the area, it was dependable, and who would be looking for an escapee in an old Camry?

THE PRESIDENT'S PAPERS

The car started up right away and I drove towards the town of Yauco, and from there I picked up the A-52 Luis Ferrer expressway to San Juan. I was apprehensive and kept looking back, sure that I had been spotted, but no one was tailing me and I reached our San Juan base within two hours. I had called ahead and explained what had happened to Gina. We both had the same question. How had the intruders avoided detection with the security measures we had in place? Even before I arrived a team had been sent to the Guanica base. Stu & five others had gone heavily armed and prepared, in 3 separate vehicles and along with them was an AH-64 Apache helicopter, which took off from the former Ramey Air Force base as an escort (on paper it wasn't supposed to exist). If anybody was there, and they were foolish enough to shoot at our guys, they were going to get whomped pretty hard. When I arrived at the San Juan office, the team had almost reached their destination. About thirty minutes later they confirmed their arrival.

Predictively, there was no one at the compound. A further analysis of the site quickly discovered that a large section of the outside perimeter warning system had been disabled at the point of entry even though the hard wiring for the system was buried twelve inches underground. They had known exactly where to dig. Even more ominous was the fact that the frequency that transmitted the outer wireless camera images had apparently been jammed, so that we had no recorded images of the incident. Somehow they had known the exact frequency the cameras operated on. Someone had given the intruders a lot of inside information, information that was supposed to be extremely confidential.

Our forensic people started picking up the numerous casings found at the site, and started obtaining casts of footprints and tire tracks. They confirmed that the attack had been executed by five people. All wore the same type of shoe, a low cost deal from Payless, sold at thousands of outlets and untraceable. No other evidence was found. No gum wrappers, no cigarette butts, not even a fingerprint. Aside from the fact that they had missed their intended target, this had been a very professional setup. Who could gather together so much firepower, and so much knowledge of our operation? And finally, who would want me killed, and for what reason? It wasn't hard to surmise that I was getting too close for comfort to locating the possessor of the missing memos.

29

I decided to remain at the San Juan office until we cleared up the identity of who was behind the assassination attempt at Guanica. I would once again be working in close proximity to Gina, but if that was torture, then I was a masochist. Stu and two of his team volunteered to keep watch of the Guanica facilities in the meantime, and the other team members were back with us in a matter of hours. Now we had to put our thinking caps and do some serious analysis of the situation, but first I had to bring Mr. Gardner up to date on the situation. As I reached for the phone I thought of something and I drew back.

There seemed to be a lot of CIA involvement in all the occurrences. Santini, the importer had at one time been used as a translator. Marole, was a thief that again, had been used at times by the Company, and then there was the fact that when I was at the Guanica compound, someone had to have had the knowledge of how to circumvent or override our base security. It didn't add up. Maybe there was a leak at Gardner's office. Maybe he had confided in the wrong person. I expressed my thoughts and worries to Gina. She listened carefully and replied,

"You could be on to something; then again you could be just totally over suspicious."

"Well just think about it. Everything can't be just one giant coincidence."

"I guess you're right, there's just to many things that just don't add up. So what do we do?"

"We set up a trap; we set up a rat trap."

"And just what do you propose?"

"Well, what do you need when you go hunting? You need two things, you need bait and a trap."

"Well we would have to get some kind of bait that would be so attractive to them that they would come out of hiding."

"Exactly, and what can be more enticing than me?"

"Well somebody thinks highly of himself, or as expressed in the language of the common man, someone is full of himself."

I smiled at her.

"You're just taking this the wrong way. What I mean is, somehow I think I've stepped on somebody's toes and they want me dead. So how about if I place myself in a vulnerable position, an open target, a sitting duck?"

"*You* want to be the bait?" she asked in surprise.

"It's the only way to draw them out."

"That would be way too dangerous. You can't do that."

"See, this is why the Company frowns upon interagency relationships. It distorts the way we see each other and gets in the way of the things that have to be done." I replied, a parody of what she had told me previously.

"Very funny, so someone is trying to kill you, and you want to present yourself as a sitting target, and that's the only rational way to solving this problem. Is that what you're saying?"

"Well, you're oversimplifying things, but yes, I guess that's what I'm saying."

I could see her looking at me and her eyes were beginning to swell with tears.

"Fine! Do whatever you think is best!"

With that she turned and walked briskly out of the office. I looked at the closed door from where she had departed for a long time and then reached for the phone to call Stewart, Manny, Eleazar, and the others to coordinate what we were going to do. We had several things to work on.

"The first thing we have to do," I told the guys who were watching me around the conference table, "is to draw them out. Like I said before, the best way to do it is by offering myself as a target, but only under controlled circumstances. I would like to be able to survive."

There were grins around the table.

"What do you have in mind?" Manny asked.

"Right now, nothing. That's why I asked you guys in. Between all of us, we should come up with a workable plan."

"Well let's get to it." Eleazar chimed in. He was always a hands on type of person.

In a few hours more than a dozen plans or suggestions had been discussed and discarded, all the while, as I listened to the discussions, I was thinking that if the leak came out of this group,

I was setting myself for an extremely dangerous, probably lethal situation. Maybe I was being paranoid, maybe not. Time would tell.

After another hour or so, we had come up with a feasible plan, and after yet another hour we had everything coordinated, and everyone had been given their assignment, and we left to start to prepare the trap.

30

In reality, there were two plans. The one I had discussed with the staff, and my private alternate twist. I figured that if there was a leak in the chain to Mr. Gardner, they would act on what was discussed and on what we had decided, but they couldn't guess the alternate twist on the events, because I was the only one who knew about it. It was the only way to protect myself while still trying to see if there really was a leak by trying to draw out the person or persons unknown who had access to the information and acted against us for unknown reasons.What we finally devised was really quite simple. I called Mr. Gardner and updated him on what had transpired until now. I let him know that I was going to Arecibo again the next day, to re-interview Andres, the contact who ran the ice-cream shop, to see if I had overlooked any important detail. He asked if I was going to go with any other team member and I said no, it was just a routine re-interview. "Be careful then."

"I will"

"And let me know any detail as soon as you get it."

"Yes sir, I will."

And with that he hung up. I didn't tell him that six other team members were already there mounting a discreet surveillance operation on the ice cream shop both on a closed net with men in nearby buildings and on foot with a broader loose mobile net. The trap was set, and I was beginning to have my suspicions on who the rat was.

The next day, I arose early, put on my bright red dress shirt and black slacks, and made the fifty minute trip to Arecibo. I arrived and found a parking space on *Calle Betances*, just off the main plaza. I got out of the car and stretched my arms over my head, a signal to my men that I had arrived, and to be alert. I slowly made my way to the plaza, crossed it and entered Andres' ice cream shop. He had an employee attend the front while we went into the back and made small talk for about half an hour. When I had judged that sufficient time had passed, I got up, took off my red shirt and revealed a white polo shirt underneath. Likewise, I took off my slacks, and revealed a pair of blue jeans. Emilio, who had been in the back room with us, and who had my same general height and physical appearance, stepped out of the shop with Andres, dressed in a red dress shirt and black slacks, and sunglasses, headed towards the car I had left parked off the plaza side street.

As Andres and I watched, we saw two gentlemen, get up from one of the plaza benches and start to converge on Emilio. They had been picked up three of my men, who themselves started converging on the original threesome. One of the two all of a sudden said something into Andres's ear and we saw the bulge of a gun at his back. Meanwhile, all three of my men had reached the group. Suddenly I stepped out in plain sight and announced, "He's not who you're looking for!"

The two pursuers looked my way, recognized me and stopped dead in their tracks, momentarily dumbfounded. At the same time, two of my men converged, gun in hand, on the duo. One of them made a snap decision to shoot Andres. It was the wrong decision. As soon as he took aim, my two men shot him, killing him instantly. Andres, meantime, had whipped out his gun and along with my third team member held the second would be kidnapper at bay, and wisely, this one dropped the gun and raised his arms in surrender. Slowly without attracting attention, a tan Ford Explorer, slipped out of its parking spot down the street, and left with its two remaining occupants, who had observed the whole scene.

By this time, we had a number of local observers, and more were arriving as the news of a killing in the plaza spread. We handcuffed our prisoner, and marched him out of there quickly. When the local police arrived, I asked to speak to my buddy, Fulgencio Jimenez, and as soon as I was put into communication with him, he said he would be right over. He arrived not ten minutes later, and soon me and my men were allowed to leave. He worked his magic and temporarily extracted us from the situation. There would probably be an investigation into the incident and some type of preliminary hearings about the event, but we had the best lawyers in the business, and they would take care of it.

We took off with the prisoner after negotiations with Mr. Jimenez. He would be needed to testify on what had happened in the plaza, but we worked out an arrangement to return the unidentified prisoner to local justice after we had a chance to interrogate him. Everything had gone off without a hitch. Now we had a possible information source, but more to the point, I might have a conduit to meeting the person or persons behind this all.

31

The call I expected came about an hour after the capture of our prisoner. Emilio came to me with the phone. He knew it was the big one.

"It's for you." He said solemnly as he scrutinized my face.

I took the phone from him. I knew the guys in the other room already had the recording and monitoring equipment on and were listening in.

"Hello? Matt here."

"Hello Mr. Hines."

"Have we talked before?"

"No, I don't believe I've had the pleasure."

"And just do I owe this honor to?"

"We don't have to play games Mr. Hines, I'm calling because you have something of mine."

"Yes, I do."

"I assure you, he knows nothing, he will be of no use to you."

"Then why are you worried?"

"Let's just say I want to have insurance. I don't like any loose ends."

"So what you're saying is that although he may know nothing, there's a possibility that he may tie you in to someone who does."

There was a pause after I said that, and I knew I had hit on something.

After a second's pause, the voice said in an ominous tone

"You must release him, or the memos will be disclosed to the media and that would not make you look good."

"So what do you propose?"

"I'm a reasonable man Mr. Hines. What I propose, as you put it, is a simple exchange, my man for the memos."

"That sounds simple enough, but I would have to call you back with the arrangements for exchange."

"The exchange is going to happen under my terms. I anticipated that you would be willing to come to terms, so I have made all the necessary plans. Listen very carefully as I will not repeat myself. We will meet next Tuesday, at 9:00 am in El Yunque at the top of the Yokahu tower. I must insist that only you and your prisoner come, no one else. I will know if you are not alone. "

"I don't think that..."

I realized that I was talking into a dead phone.

I looked up at Manny; the meeting was set for Tuesday.

"We have a lot of work to do."

32

"El Yunque", is a tropical rainforest in the northwest part of the island. Covering 28,000 acres and the only tropical rainforest in the U.S. National Forest System, it started life in 1876 when Puerto Rico was still a Spanish colony and King Alfonso XII declared it a forest reserve. Its status as a preservation area was reconfirmed by Theodore Roosevelt in 1903 when Puerto Rico passed into U.S. hands. Expansion, seeding, added trails, and the building of a visitor's center in 1996, made it the popular tourist destination it is today.

Rain clouds constantly cover the highest peaks of the rain forest most days. It is very humid. On a surveillance mission a couple of years ago, I had taken a video camera and to my surprise, it had shorted out with the moisture, rendering the camera, the tape, and the mission useless. The forest is crisscrossed by five different established hiking trails, and there are two observation towers with panoramic views of the surrounding forest. From these, on clear days, there is visibility clear to the coast and the Atlantic Ocean beyond. My rendezvous had been scheduled in one of these towers. It was called the Yokahu tower, and it sat near the main entrance of the preserve.

PEDRO VARGAS

Whoever had chosen the meeting site had not chosen well. It was true that the area was extensive, and it would be practically impossible to mount an effective surveillance. The person would also have a bird's eye view of anyone approaching, and a clear view of any aerial approach. There was one major weak point, there was only one road in and out of the area. We could have visual control of anyone coming or going. I set up a team at the main entrance road, and risked placing three of our operatives, posing as tourists, in the general area, with instructions of not communicating unless a dire emergency came up since I didn't know if the channels would be monitored by my mysterious "host". I was going to get aerial surveillance help. Manny had a contact with the local Coast Guard and had made the proper arrangements. It seemed that everything was set.

33

I looked down from Yokahu tower. I saw an impossibly green expanse of vegetation roll out onto the horizon where it met an impossibly blue sky. Living on the island you got used to these colors, but once in a while you had brief moments of free time where your concentration was unfettered and you could drink in and appreciate the beauty of this natural paradise.

I had arrived with my handcuffed prisoner a few minutes early. I wanted to avoid any surprises if I could. The early morning sun wasn't in full force and the temperature was still very cool. Apparently, I had not gotten up early enough for suddenly I heard a voice behind me.

"Good morning Mr. Hines!"

I instantly recognized it. Turning around quickly, I confirmed my suspicion. It was who I thought it was.

"Mr. Gardner!"

"A little shocked to see me, eh Matt?"

"You? What are you doing here?"

"You don't get it Matt, do you?, I'm the one who set up this meeting."

"You! Why?"

"Let's just say I have to protect my interests." as he pulled a Colt 45 from his pocket and trained it on me.

"I don't understand."

"Matt, Matt, so trusting. Let me be clear, I am protecting a memo, but the memo I'm protecting has nothing to do with the Kennedy assassination."

"So it's something that implicates you, and it really doesn't have any political implications."

"Very good! I'm impressed. You're right in the fact that it implicates me, but there would still be serious, very serious, international repercussions if the contents of the memo were made known."

"What are we talking about?" I asked, very leery of the gun pointed in my direction.

"You didn't believe that hogwash about the Babushka lady did you?"

I felt a little hurt because I had, but I remained silent.

"Poor little Robert, at least you deserve to know the truth before you die."

"I'm not going to die" I replied, "the park is under surveillance, you're going to get caught."

Gardner just smiled. There was a movement from the shadow of the staircase behind him and suddenly a figure spilled out into the sunlight, gun in hand.

"Manny!" I gasped in surprise.

Manny took a position opposite that of Gardner. He was at my two o'clock and Gardner at my ten o'clock. It was smart of them not to be bunched together, but being that Manny had the gun pointed directly at me, the move seemed unnecessary.

"I seems Matt that the troops won't be rallying to the rescue after all."

Manny gave me a sarcastic smile,

"Sorry boss, but I had to go with the money."

I just gave Manny an icy look. I had never had an inkling of a thought of betrayal from him.

34

"**N**ow that you're fate is sealed, as I was saying, you deserve to know the truth." Gardner continued.

"Yes, I killed Golitsin and have the missing notes. In reality, Matt, the real story has to do with money. You see, in 1959 I was a young start-up under Dulles, with patriotic stars in my eyes, but I always had a taste for the finer things in life. I had several demanding girlfriends then. A couple of months into my job I was asked about my father. He was a biogeneticist who had been sent to work in a laboratory in a small village called Ebolawa in Cameroon, Africa. He had always been deliberately vague on what he actually did. The only details that I was able to gather were that he was collaborating on a secret government project, and that it had to do with a study on pathogens. I later found out the details, a lot of details. It seems that dear old dad had, under the auspices of the American government, worked on developing a strain of virus that would be immune to any current medical therapy. In other words he was developing a biological weapon. He eventually, through a lot of trial and error, developed a virus that seemed to fit the parameters that were wanted.

He was anxious to test it and started doing so with chimpanzees. All was going well until the unthinkable happened. One night one of the cleaning personnel realized that one of the lab doors was open. He had expressly been told to never enter the lab area even if, as in this case, he found it unlocked. Curiosity got the better of him though, and he went in. He was surprised to see a row of chimps in cages. He cautiously approached them because they seemed to look so harmless and forlorn. One in particular, attracted his attention and he went to its cage and put his finger through to pet it when, in a sudden motion, the chimp turned and bit him hard. He screamed out in pain, and in an instinctive motion pulled back his hand toppling the cage to the floor where it landed with a crash, opening the hinged cage door. The captive chimp rushed out and escaped. The terrified cleaning person kept quiet about the incident. A year later this person acquired enough money to start his own small store and left the lab and went into business on his own. In about this time frame, he started experimenting strange symptoms. He started having cold sweats, fevers, etc. He went to the local doctor, who was at a loss to explain the symptoms, and gave him antibiotics. When these did not work, he went to a Bamileke shaman who did goat sacrifices and other rituals on his behalf trying to save him, but of course, these were ineffective and he died. He was quietly buried on his family's property. Soon, various other villagers presented the same symptoms and also died fairly quickly. A large local family, sensing that a contagious disease seemed to be amongst their midst moved to Kinshasa, far away from the outbreak, not knowing the disease had come with them, and so it spread, through Africa and then beyond.

We realized we had a problem, when the CDC heard rumors of the many deaths and started investigating. The Department of Defense soon realized that their experimental virus had somehow leaked out and they rushed to eradicate all signs of their presence, including the untimely death of some of the principals. Dear dad had passed away but I was assigned some of the clean-up operations although I wasn't given details on the targets or why they were to be eliminated. I was just told that they were a threat to national security and I did not question it. I arranged with professionals in the field to have them disappear. This then, is my dirty little secret, the real subject of the missing memos, the one, my friend, you are going to die for."

With that, he started to point his gun at me and I braced for the impact.

At that same instant I heard a shot and I saw Mr. Gardner's gun disintegrate. Another shot rang out, so close to the first one that it sounded as one. A look of disbelief crossed Manny's face as a darkish red stain rapidly spread on his chest. He fell slowly to his knees and then collapsed on the floor. Before I could react, Gardner, holding his injured hand, had run towards the exit and had shoved Gina aside violently, causing her to fall, and rushed down the stairs.

I ran to Gina's side, "Are you alright?"

She grimaced at me but answered, "I just hit my tailbone and it hurts like the dickens, but I'll be alright. Help me get up."

I grasped her hand and pulled her up.

"We have to go after him!" she yelled as she turned to run to the stairs. She was limping as she went. I knew enough to not try to stop her. I followed her into the semi-dark staircase and we started to descend as quickly as possible. As I pulled my cell phone from my pocket I asked her,

"How did you get here? How did you know where I was?"

"Someone had to protect you from yourself, so I managed to come in as a tourist last evening, a little before closing time, and I managed to keep hidden, and then I spent the night here. I figured, correctly as it turns out, that the meet would be near the entrance, and when I saw Gardner go up this tower, then you, I debated on whether I should follow immediately, and it was a good thing I did, because all of a sudden I see Manny coming up behind you two, and I had a hunch on what might be going on, so I followed, listened, and confirmed my suspicions. I waited for an appropriate opportunity to burst in, and you know the rest."

As we reached the bottom and exited the tower, I reached down in a tuft of grass at the entrance and retrieved a mini trans receiver I had hidden there on my way in. I didn't know if I was going to be scanned, so I hadn't taken the risk. Now I screamed into it,

"The mark is Mr. Gardner, the mark is Mr. Gardner! Manny was also in on it but he's been put down at the Yokahu tower. Manny was dirty. Send choppers and men! Saturate the area! I repeat, saturate the area immediately!"

Almost instantly, I heard the chop-chop of the blades of the first helicopter approaching the area. A report came in from the chopper.

"I have a visual, he's apparently trying to make Pico East, there's a white SUV on the access road there. We can send people to block that."

"Roger that, I'm heading that way."

"We're also trying to get a National Guard contingent to you, but that has to go through some hoops and barrels, but we're trying to expedite that as much as possible. Meanwhile, I'll maintain a visual."

"Thank you, you efforts and help are acknowledged."

I glanced over at Gina, both she and I were gasping, the altitude was getting to us, but we pushed onward. I didn't want to miss out on the capture.

"I don't think I can make it, you keep on!" Gina gasped.

"Let's take a minute and then we'll keep on together." I managed to gasp out."

With that Gina leaned over and put her hands on her knees and tried to catch her breath. I did the same. My only consolation in the situation was that Garner was probably even more out of shape than we were and was probably doing the same.

A crackle came over my headset, then,

"He broke out of the brush at the El Pico road and apparently spotted the car we have there. He doubled back. I can't see him because he's using the ground cover to stay concealed and the visibility is almost zero because of the cloud cover, but I can give you a read on his direction with the infrared."

I looked up. In the haste of the chase, I hadn't noticed the gray clouds racing in. Almost on cue, it started drizzling. Gina and I welcomed the water. It refreshed us from the stifling heat. The air was thick with water vapor, and the musky smell of the vegetation was intensified. All of a sudden, the drizzle turned into a torrential rain. The sound of the falling rain drowned out every other sound. The helicopter pilot broke in.

"I'm ineffective right now; I have zero visibility so I'm going to have to back out. The subject was last seen heading towards the area of Mt. Britton."

"Roger that," I replied, " Make sure a perimeter be set as tight as possible around the area, especially around the main entrance, and at the service road, and tell everyone to keep on their toes, the subject is armed."

"Will do our best, but the rain will make it very difficult."

"I'm close by. We'll try to find him, over and out."

I knew what the pilot meant. This type of rain created instant flooding in areas, and also, there was the danger of mudslides, which were common after rains of this intensity, and which could block the only road in.

35

"He's headed toward Mt. Britton!" I yelled at Gina. I had to raise my voice to be heard over the roar of the rainfall.

"OK, let's go!" she replied. We were soaked and miserable, but the excitement of the hunt made us pay scarce attention to our personal situation.

I was puzzled as to Gardner's direction of travel. All there was in that direction was another observation tower appropriately named the Mt. Britton tower and beyond that you reached the highest mountain points in the rainforest. It was a virtual dead end. Maybe he was thinking of disappearing into the forest and trying to emerge at an open point. That would be foolish and dangerous. Without food or supplies, and with the approaching night-time and the torrential rain, he could get lost and even die. It had happened several times in the past already. I was sloshing through a pool of water when suddenly Gina grabbed my arm, and yelled to be heard over the roar of the downpour,

"There he is!"

I looked in the direction she was pointing, and although it was hard to see because of the pelting rain, sure enough, there he was, a lone miserable looking figure, in the distance, water dripping from his hair and clothes, stumbling and struggling to keep on.

As if he had a premonition, he suddenly stopped and turned, and saw us. He realized he had been spotted, and he seemed to recognize me. This seemed to give him a burst of energy and he turned and disappeared into the mist and greenery of the trail he was on.

Gina and I raced on trying to catch another glimpse. The rain made it very difficult. Finally, at a distance, and through the mist, I saw him. I put my hand on Gina's shoulder as a signal, and pointed in his direction. She saw him too. He had passed the turnoff trail to the Mt. Britton tower, the second of the observation towers in the rainforest. At first, I had thought he was headed for the tower, but then realized he was heading towards the highest parts of the rainforest and he was trying to disappear into the vegetation, which frankly, was his only remaining alternative. As I watched, I could see him stumble and sometimes fall in the now slippery, wet trail. At times, because of the poor visibility, I would momentarily lose sight of him.

Suddenly a sound that seemed like thunder reached my ears. Great, I thought, that's all I needed. It added another dimension of danger to an already arduous pursuit.

We were gaining on Gardner. I now had a constant visual on him. His age and lack of physical conditioning were slowing him down considerably. I could see him gasping for air, but forcing himself to go on. We redoubled our efforts. I turned to help Gina up a slight incline and just then I heard an ominous rumble that could be heard even over the roar of the copious rainfall. I thought at first that it was another clap of thunder, but I realized that the noise seemed to have direction and get closer. I glanced over at Gina, and her face reflected the same puzzled look I had on mine. All of a sudden I felt as if someone had grabbed me by the ankles and had tackled me, and then everything turned black.

36

I started sensing the rain again, but also an incredible, familiar, and very comforting warmth. I also heard soft sobbing, and felt comforting hands. Then I heard my name called, over and over. I must be in a beautiful dream I thought, for the voice and touch felt like Gina's. Then I drifted into a higher level of awareness and slowly opened my eyes, and realized it was Gina. She was a surprising sight, caked in mud, I could only make out her eyes but nonetheless, it was her.

"Gina." I managed to mumble.

She peered into my face with red swollen eyes, and tears streaming down her face.

"Oh, Matt! You're alive!"

With that she kissed me several times in a hungrily passionate way. If I had died at that very moment, I would have not regretted my life at all.

EPILOGUE

We had barely escaped with our lives. It seems that we had been standing at the outer edge of one of the worst mudslides in the park's history. It had knocked me over and I had hit a rock that had caused a concussion and knocked me unconscious. Gina was also knocked down, but fell into the edge of the mudslide and had managed to escape, aside from scrapes and bruises, relatively unharmed. She had waded through the mess towards me and found me nearby, and had, with great effort dragged me out of harm's way, saving my life.

Mr. Garner had made good his escape; into the hereafter. His body was found downslope from where we had last seen him, several days later, with the help of cadaver dogs. On searching his office, later on, we found the notes and they were destroyed. Not many went to his funeral. I was there. For some odd reason, I felt compelled to go. I didn't know what to say to Margie, his widow, so we just embraced, for a minute, and then I walked awkwardly away. Gina had gone with me, and she put her arm around me, and helped me past the confusion and dreariness of that moment, and of the days that followed.

Oh yes; Gina. We were together once more. Our near death experience had torn away the curtains of foolishness, self-importance, and self-pride, from both of us. I especially had glimpsed what was really important to me; and I realized it was her. She gave me a second chance, and I intended to make the most of it.

THE END